Jack Vance
The Deadly Isles

Jack Vance

The
Deadly
Isles

John Halbrok Vance

Jack Vance

The Deadly Isles

CHAPTER I

FROM THE SOCIAL NEWS of the *San Francisco Chronicle*,
November 20, 1967:

LIA WINTERSEA ANNOUNCES TROTH
TO YACHTSMAN BRADY ROYCE

At a Saint Francis Hotel luncheon Lia Wintersea told six close friends of her engagement to popular socialite and yachtsman Brady Royce. Lia is daughter of the talented oboeist Paul Wintersea, who plays with the San Francisco Symphony, and Maude Ridlow Wintersea, an accomplished pianist in her own right. Lia's sister Jean is a flautist of professional caliber who instead of a career in music has chosen the field of industrial psychology to make her mark.

The wedding will take place in the late spring at Golconda, the fabled Royce town house, and will be followed by a cruise aboard Brady's schooner *Dorado IV* to remote and romantic islands in the South Seas.

Present at the luncheon were Lia's sister Jean, Kelsey McClure, Mrs. Christian deBrouf (Peggy Satterlee)...

From the *San Francisco Examiner*,
January 26, 1968:

DANCER TORTURED, STRANGLED;
APARTMENT RIFLED

Inez Gallegos, 23, a specialty dancer employed by the Martinique, 619 Ellis Street, this morning was found dead in her apartment at

1526 Powell Street. She had been strangled with a stocking. On her face, neck, legs and body were numerous burns, inflicted with a cigar, according to Detective Inspector William Reinhold.

The body was discovered at 11:10 A.M. by Richard B. Cody, 34, a bartender at the Polka Dot Bar, 320 O'Farrell Street, who had come to take Miss Gallegos to breakfast.

The apartment had been ransacked; Miss Gallegos' purse and belongings had been rifled but she apparently had not been subjected to sexual assault.

Cody states that a metal document box containing Miss Gallegos' birth certificate, car ownership certificate and other papers is missing.

CHAPTER II

BRADY ROYCE, AT FORTY-EIGHT, was heavy-shouldered, a trifle ungainly, with overlarge features, a heavy jaw and mouth, coarse dark hair thinning across the scalp: not a handsome or even a distinguished-appearing man; but, in the words of his friend Dorothy McClure: "With money like Brady's got, who needs looks?" Brady's humor was broad and sometimes unkind, but generally his bark was worse than his bite and his friends liked him in spite of his faults. His enemies thought him obstinate, domineering, peevish, narrow-minded, unsympathetic.

Brady's engagement to Lia Wintersea gave rise to predictable sniffs: "Dear Brady. Who'd ever think he'd go all senile, gamboling with pretty young things and all?" When such remarks were brought to Brady's attention he only smiled with grim complacence. Lia was as extravagantly beautiful as Brady was wealthy, and if the marriage derived from considerations other than mutual rapture, each party seemed satisfied with the contract.

Lia, while she looked a year or two younger than her twenty-two years, was a woman of poise, charm and dignity. She was deliciously shaped, supple and slender, with an ease of motion that was almost musical. From a Spanish grandmother came rich black hair, Castilian complexion, a look of latent Spanish passion; a Welsh grandfather gave her eyes of magic grey. Lia was casual and low-key; she never preened nor wore exhibitionistic clothes, and achieved an effortless elegance. Brady's friends scrutinized her with care. Some commended her lack of vanity, others suspected reverse arrogance; Lia would have recognized herself in neither point of view. She was herself, just as she had been all her life, with her unique and particular problems. She had no delusions regarding the marriage, though she rather liked Brady and thought him virile and masterful. She might have liked him even had he not been wealthy.

By the San Francisco time-scale the Royces were an old family, having arrived shortly after the Gold Rush.

In 1859 at Bodie, Nevada, a hobo named Ham Royce filled an inside straight and won three demonstrably worthless mining claims near Virginia City (although a man named Comstock thought he had detected silver nearby). Of the two hundred and twenty million dollars yielded by the Comstock Lode, Ham Royce took thirty million.

Easy come, easy go, but not for Ham Royce. He invested in farmlands, cattle, railroad stock, real estate. Money came so easily that by 1880 the zest was gone. Ham Royce, one-time hobo, traveled to Europe. At Fiesole he admired the Villa Portinari, which, so it happened, was not for sale. Ham Royce tapped a pencil against his yellow old teeth, drew a set of sketches in his notebook, despatched a shipload of Carrara marble, rugs, candelabra, tapestries, Hellenistic urns, Spanish armour, early Italian paintings, antique oak beams and walnut paneling to San Francisco, where, on Pacific Heights, with a clear view from the Golden Gate to Yerba Buena Island, he built Golconda.

In 1890 he acquired the first *Dorado*, a sea-going yawl, which he sailed to the Aleutians for the purpose of hunting Kodiak bear.

Ham's only son was William. At the age of twenty William drank too much champagne and married a chorus girl. The experience had much to recommend it; a week later William drank more champagne and married another chorus girl. Ham Royce declared both marriages null and void and sent William off to Japan on the *Dorado*.

Ham Royce now gave serious thought to the future. The episode had cost relatively little: a hundred thousand to each of the girls, another twenty or thirty thousand in incidental expenses — but William was not a satisfactory son. He had never worked a day in his life; he condescended toward his father; he could not hold his liquor. Ham walked gloomily around Golconda, wondering what would become of his wonderful Italian palace when William was able to drink all the champagne he liked. Ham, a man predisposed toward extreme solutions, acted immediately. He paid the totality of his wealth into a trust fund dedicated to the maintenance of Golconda and its various adjuncts, such as the *Dorado*. The administrator he stipulated to be that legally sane, legitimately born Royce in the line of succession as established by the English common law schedule of primogeniture. A spouse would qualify as 'resident administrator' only when consanguinity to the third degree had been exhausted. For personal expenses the 'resident administrator' drew upon the income of the fund, but was subject to a set of provisions which made his remuneration precisely equal to his expenses. Legally the administrator was a pauper; practically he was a millionaire. William could drink champagne, he could marry chorus girls as he chose, at their own risk. When it came time to sue, William could truthfully assert that he was allowed no funds for any such contingencies. By this means Ham hoped to protect William against himself and to preserve Golconda against sequestration and folly.

William's two sons were Philip and Lemuel. Philip, upon becoming administrator, urged that Lemuel continue to make his home at Golconda. Lemuel refused and sued for a share of the estate, claiming that the Golconda Fund constituted an illegal entail. The courts decided otherwise. Lemuel moved south to La Jolla and never returned to San Francisco. His son Luke, less inflexible, was a frequent visitor to Golconda during his undergraduate years at the University of California and crewed aboard both *Dorado III* and *Dorado IV*.

Philip's only son Brady began his career as a typical Royce. He married Hortense Lejeune, a French cinema star, by whom he bred a son, Carson, then, at a scandalous trial, divorced her for flagrant adultery. Hortense haughtily returned to France, leaving Carson, the future administrator, in Brady's custody.

For a dozen years Brady reigned as San Francisco's most eligible bachelor. Then, at the home of his friend Malcolm McClure, Kelsey McClure introduced him to Lia Wintersea.

The marriage of Brady Royce to Lia Wintersea on May 10, 1968, was the grandest event of the season. The guest list defined San Francisco quality; and those who felt that they should have been, but were not, invited found compelling reasons why they could not be on hand: excursions to Europe, conferences in Washington, in one instance a canoe trip down the Athabasca River to the Great Slave Lake.

The ceremony took place in the ballroom at Golconda. The reception was lavish beyond the experience of anyone present: like his great-grandfather Ham, when Brady Royce did something, he did it right. The honeymoon would be in the same scale: a week at Brady's lodge in the Sawtooth Mountains, then an extended cruise aboard the *Dorado IV*, touching at Honolulu, the Marquesas Islands, Tahiti, and wherever else the winds blew: Rarotonga? Samoa? Bali? The Philippines? One was as likely as the other, declared Brady.

Aboard the *Dorado IV* would be a number of guests: Carson, now nineteen; Jim and Nancy Crothers; Malcolm and Dorothy McClure; their daughter Kelsey, who had introduced Lia to Brady; Don Pepper-gold, a young attorney to whom Brady had taken a fancy. At Honolulu Jim and Nancy Crothers would leave the party, while Lia's sister Jean would come aboard, as would Brady's cousin Luke at Tahiti.

The wedding proceeded with the pomp and pageantry of a coronation; the bride by general agreement was the most beautiful woman ever to become a Royce. Malcolm McClure was Brady's best man; the single bridesmaid was Jean Wintersea, who appeared pinched and colorless beside her white jade, rose and jet sister.

The reception followed; Lia cut an enormous cake, then she and Jean slipped away to change clothes.

Lia seemed listless and wan — even dejected. Jean, two years older than Lia, and well-acquainted with her sister's temperament, felt completely baffled.

After the maids carried off the wedding gown Lia dropped upon a couch to stare out the window. Jean watched a careful moment, then seated herself beside her sister. "What on earth is the matter? You act as if you're headed for a concentration camp!"

Lia grimaced, gave her hands a nervous little shake. "Don't be silly."

"Better show a little more enthusiasm when you're with Brady," warned Jean, "or he'll think you don't like him."

Lia drew a deep breath. "I like him well enough. It's not that. In fact, he's very considerate." She put her chin in her hands. "The truth is shocking. I'm three months pregnant. Now you know."

"Good heavens," breathed Jean. "By Brady, I hope?"

Lia gave a bitter laugh. "That's the tragic part... It's that wretched you-know-who."

Jean considered a long moment, watching her sister sidelong. Then she said, "I thought that was all over long ago."

"I thought so too," said Lia in a dreary voice. "It wasn't my idea."

"But *why*?" demanded Jean. "It's incredible! It's insane!"

Lia gave another bitter little laugh. "I couldn't help it. He made me. I guess I don't have much will-power."

"I still don't understand. How could he make you? Do you mean force?"

Lia considered a moment. "No. Not exactly. I don't want to talk about it. Really."

"Poor little Lia." Jean gave her sister a slow frowning inspection, while Lia, chewing at her lip, stared out the window.

Lia said, "If Brady found out — after a six months' engagement — he'd be very upset. He'd be worse than upset. Do you know," she spoke in hushed wonder, "he's actually quite strait-laced!"

"You'll have to get rid of it," said Jean flatly.

"I know," said Lia. "But where? Aboard the *Dorado*? With a belaying pin? Or a boat-hook? Whatever they're called."

"Why didn't you have it done before?"

"I wasn't sure till a couple weeks ago. I missed the second month. After that — well, I didn't have time. There was so much to do."

"It doesn't show. You'll be in Honolulu in two or three weeks. Have it done there."

"Yes," said Lia. "I suppose I'll have to... You could telephone me that Mother was sick, and I'd fly back to San Francisco for a few days."

"He'd want to come with you: dutiful new husband and all."

"I suppose he would... Oh, heavens, how do I ever get in such messes?"

"I know how," said Jean with a grim smile. "But it wouldn't do any good to tell you."

*

On May 30th Jean received a letter from Lia, postmarked May 29th, at Honolulu:

Well, we arrived. Intact. The ship is beautiful; all are very nice, though puzzled. I blame everything on seasickness. Carson is a brat, and very cynical. He won't keep his hands off Kelsey, who is bored with him. I've made a few discreet inquiries, but I can't find anything except some Chinese herb doctors. If nothing this afternoon I may have to fly back to San Francisco. Brady is visiting Kona for a few days, to look at a coffee plantation somebody wants to sell him. I told him I wanted to do some shopping and recover from my seasickness, so I'll be staying at the Royal Hawaiian.

Kelsey is visiting friends and will not get to Kona either. I wouldn't be surprised if she suspects things. She looks at me with a funny half-grin. If I could only find a you-know-what! In San Francisco there wouldn't be any trouble. I wonder how long I'd be sick? Maybe I could fly over and fly right back. Well, we shall see. I'll go to the beauty salon; they always know about these things. Important! Brady has set departure date for June 6. He's very stern about such matters; he thinks he's a sea-captain or something. Anyway, plan to be here by the 5th or earlier. Try the Royal Hawaiian first, then the Kamehameha Yacht Club.

Love,
Lia

Sard's was situated south of Market at 69 Homan Street, half-way along a disreputable alley, between the Embarcadero and the railroad yards: not a fashionable district, but then Sard's clientele was, by and large, not a fashionable crowd. The façade was self-consciously smart: heavy squares of earth-colored Mexican tile set in rough black grout. There was a door of iron-bound oak, and SARD's spelled out in small black back-lit letters.

Within all was different — or perhaps the same? The bar, the tables, the chairs, the walls — all were rude and rough, as if the proprietor had sought to reproduce an old cow-town saloon. The effect was accentuated by carefully dramatic lighting, and the room seemed more like a stage-set than a tavern.

The patrons were almost exclusively young men, some with low side-burns, others with drooping mustaches, others with heads shaved bald. Excessively tight trousers with heavy leather belts were much in evidence, and two persons wore boots with spurs. Almost everyone drank straight Scotch and stood at the bar, thumbs hooked in belts, legs splayed. One wall was vivid with bullfight posters; at the back of the bar was a human skull in a Reichswehr helmet, a red rose clenched between the teeth.

At nine o'clock on the night of Sunday, June 2nd, a strange-looking woman came into Sard's bar. Her face was unnaturally white; her hair was pulled tightly back under a black scarf. She wore a long black coat, large dark glasses; her mouth was a black smear of lipstick. Just inside the entrance she paused to look along the bar. Failing to find whom she sought she went to a table at the back wall. Only two other women were present: a pair of thin nervous blondes with bushes of teased hair. They sat at a table with two young bucks in black turtleneck sweaters, and all took turns telling dirty jokes.

The men standing along the bar turned appraising looks at the woman in the black coat, then shrugged and gave her no further attention.

She sat an hour sipping gin and tonic. Patrons departed, others swaggered in. Voices rose; there was much boisterous laughter.

At twenty minutes to eleven the woman in black leaned quickly forward. The man who had just entered was tall, broad of shoulder, lean of hip; he wore tight beige trousers, a black cap, black shoes, a tight black sport shirt, open at the neck. He was an extremely handsome man, with dark hair, a splendid jaw and chin, a high-bridged nose. His cheek-bones were perhaps a trifle dull; his eyes, which were a remarkable black, were perhaps over-bright and somewhat too close together; but these flaws, if such they were, detracted little from the overall effect. He was as dramatic as his setting; he carried himself like a character in a silent movie, a synthesis of Douglas Fairbanks, John Gilbert, Ramon Navarro.

The woman in black signaled to him. He stared, then crossed the room with an incredulous expression on his face. "Good God, the disguise! I didn't recognize you."

"I didn't want to be recognized."

"No risk! What's on your mind?"

"One thing and another. How are your finances?"

The black opal eyes narrowed. "As usual, which means bad. Why? Are you distributing loot?"

"Not exactly. But sit down."

"Wait till I get a drink. What's yours?"

"Gin and tonic."

The man returned with a pair of drinks, threw a leg over the back of the chair, eased down into the seat. "Something of a surprise seeing you. I thought you were far away."

The woman in black sipped the gin and tonic. "You've been reading the society section."

"When something interesting happens."

"What about the front page?"

"I look at the headlines."

"I see where poor Inez Gallegos died."

The man raised his eyebrows in perplexity — whether real or feigned, the woman, who was now looking toward the ceiling, made no attempt to distinguish. She asked, "How would you like to make a lovely trip through the South Pacific?"

"I'd like. Who do I have to sleep with? Don't tell me. I'll go regardless."

"Be serious," said the woman. "This is a very serious situation... Very, very serious..."

CHAPTER III

LUKE ROYCE WORKED OUT of a native-style cottage in Teahupoo, on the western shore of Tahiti Iti, the small end of the Tahiti hourglass. The location was remote; the surroundings were picturesque in the extreme. Luke's front porch stood on stilts above a white beach, with his outrigger canoe drawn up above high water. Papayas, bananas, mangos and a small tart red fruit known locally as 'dragon's-eye' grew in his back yard. Cocoanut palms slanted up at all angles around the periphery of a small cove, created by a projecting point of land on one side, a cliff of volcanic rock on the other.

During the fifteen months of his residence Luke had hooked, netted and trapped thousands of fish. To the tuna, albacore and swordfish he pinned stainless steel tabs and turned them back into the sea, to the wonder of Armand Tefaatau, his assistant. A very few of these fish carried tabs affixed by other stations, and when Luke found one of these he immediately reported the circumstance to La Jolla.

Luke, twenty-eight years old, bore little resemblance to his cousin Brady, except, perhaps, for the square Royce forehead and something of the outward splay of jaw-bone which gave Brady's face a heavy Cro-Magnon cast. Luke was of medium height, good if unobtrusive physique. His disposition was even; his style of conduct tended toward understatement; the expression of his face was wry, as if everywhere he looked he found amusing contradictions. Nothing about Luke caught the eye or attracted attention except his remarkable beard: a shapeless brown scurf which owed its existence, not to ideology, but to a lost razor. The Tahitian girls found the beard fascinating. The little ones liked to tie it full of hibiscus and frangipani, and sometimes the older ones as well.

On the afternoon of Saturday, June 8, Luke started his Vespa, bumped up the rutted track to the road, turned left toward Papeete, thirty miles distant: a weekly routine. The road led along the shore, through enchanting scenery: dense forests of *mape*, ironwood, bread-fruit, pandanus, cocoanut palms leaning across beaches; dark grottoes framed by ferns and big-leaved plants; and always flowers: banks and bowers of scarlet, orange, indigo, mauve, pale blue. One by one Luke passed through the various districts, each named for the ancient tribe which had controlled it: Papeari, Mataiea, Papara, Paea, into increas-ing traffic; through Punaauia and Faaa, beside the new air-terminal, at last into the outskirts of Papeete. Luke turned off Broom Road, swung down to the Quai Bir Hakeim, parked across from the post office. Here was the central node of the South Seas. To right and left boats were moored: ketches, schooners, sloops, yawls, several trimarans; boats from San Francisco, Los Angeles, Auckland, Sydney, Acapulco, New York, Boston, Monaco, London: all drawn to Longitude 149° 33' w, Latitude 17° 33' s, by the glamour of the word 'Tahiti'. Tied up to the dock not a hundred feet from where Luke had parked was the *Rahiria*, a big inter-island trading schooner. In about a month Luke's cousin Brady would arrive at Papeete in his own schooner, about the same size as the *Rahiria*, but inexpressibly more comfortable.

Luke crossed the street to the big new glass and concrete post office. He entered the side annex in which was his box, No. 421.

On a bench beside the window-wall a dark-haired man in white shorts sat reading a newspaper. Luke might never have heeded him except for a French lady in a gaudy pareu, her small boy and her poodle. Sidling around the group, Luke met the intent gaze of a pair of glitter-ing black eyes. Surprised, Luke looked back. The man was absorbed in his newspaper.

Luke opened his box. The glass front of the box to the side reflected a somewhat distorted image of the man in white shorts, again watching Luke with a peculiar fixity.

When Luke turned Black-eyes was engrossed in his reading. Strange, thought Luke. To the best of his knowledge he had never seen the man before in his life… He went outside, looked through his letters, two of which were important. The first announced termination of the fish-migration study. Luke was instructed to close down his operations. This was a notice he had been expecting for three months, and it could not have come at a better time.

The second letter, from his cousin Brady, had been mailed at Honolulu on June 5. It read:

> *Dear Luke:*
>
> *We're making departure tomorrow. Weather cooperating, we'll raise Nuku Hiva in the Marquesas about June 24. If you can break away from your job why not join us there? There is plenty of room — comparatively speaking that is; you'll have to share a stateroom with Carson. I don't think you know anyone else aboard, except old Bill Sarvis, who is still Chief Engineer. But I assure you that it is a jolly crew.*
>
> *I propose to explore Nuku Hiva for a week, more or less, then make for Hiva Oa, which I understand to be spectacular. Everybody is in the best of spirits. If you ever marry, this is undoubtedly the proper honeymoon, although Lia had a rocky trip over from San Francisco. She is feeling much better now, much more enthusiastic, and no doubt will be taking to the nautical life like a real Royce. Her sister Jean is also with us, having come aboard yesterday. Well, I will knock this off and take care of some last minute details. We hope to see you either at Nuku Hiva or at Hiva Oa. Our first stop will be the port of entry at Taio Hae Bay, as I say about June 24. If you are not waiting for us I will leave word with the officials as to our anchorage, and also leave a letter for you.*
>
> *Regards, and see you at Papeete in any case.*
>
> *Brady*

Luke re-read the letter, tugging absently at his unsightly beard...He could close down his job in two hours. And there was the *Rahiria*, conveniently at hand. Luke walked up the street to the Vaima, the popular sidewalk café. Under gaudy parasols the tables were crowded: tourists from a Swedish cruise ship and from the hotels; Foreign Legionnaires in white caps; local French and Tahitians. The visitors watched the girls, the locals watched the tourists, each deriving amusement from the other. Luke found a seat and ordered beer. The waitress presently brought him a bottle with the familiar Hinano label: a girl caressing a flower. Automatically Luke turned the bottle around, studied the label from the reverse side, whereupon a lewd scene became evident, or so his Tahitian friends assured him. Luke had never been able to see it. A clean mind, no doubt. Perhaps stupidity...

Luke sat back, thrust out his legs. Pleasant to sit at the Vaima and watch the life of Papeete flow past. Many before him had found it so. Pleasant especially to watch the girls, some of whom were very appealing.

The time had come when he must leave Tahiti. Luke felt mingled anticipation and sadness. Out in Teahupoo the world was far away, isolated by a quality far more elemental than miles. Never again would he live so close to water and air and sunlight; his friends — the Tefaataus, the Vaita'ahuas, the Himeas, their cousins and aunts and uncles — would gradually forget him; gradually he would forget the songs and his few words of Tahitian. At Teahupoo the days passed slowly — but the months slid by with disturbing ease. A man tended to lose contact with the world. The real world? Perhaps, perhaps not: Luke wasn't sure. Still, more and more of late he had known small pangs of guilt. Perhaps someday he might return, but more likely not. The risk of anticlimax would be too great... Luke suddenly became aware that, without conscious deliberation, he had decided to meet the *Dorado* in the Marquesas. Armand could look after his belongings until he returned to Papeete.

Luke sat up in his seat, consulted his watch, looked down the street toward the blue façade of Etablissements Donald, agents for the *Rahiria*. They were now closed; Luke would have to wait until Monday before booking passage. If he were lucky he might still find a berth available. If not, he'd go deck class, like the Polynesians.

Luke drank a second bottle of beer, re-read his mail, then considered how he would spend the rest of the day. He had intended to dine at Chez Chapiteau or perhaps the Bougainville, which was quieter and cheaper and more pleasantly situated among the trees to the back of town... On the other hand, a delay meant riding the Vespa home after dark, which in the unpredictable traffic was hard on the nerves. Then there was Armand, who might be difficult to find on a Saturday night… Suddenly anxious to be on his way, Luke rose to his feet, walked up the Quai Bir Hakeim, toward his motor-scooter.

Across the street, sauntering idly in the same direction, was the man with the black eyes. The post office was a queer place to read a newspaper, thought Luke. Perhaps the fellow had been waiting for someone. The man, turning his back, paused to inspect a very ordinary boat moored to the wharf. Crossing the street Luke approached the *Rahiria* and in execrable French called up to a Tahitian deck-hand:

"*Quand partit le bateau?*"

"*Mardi, m'sieu.*"

"*Peut-être je vais aussi.*"

"*Bien. C'est un voyage agréable.*"

"*Vous allez aux îles Marquises, n'est-ce pas?*"

"*Oui, m'sieu. D'abord les îles Tuamotus: puis les Marquises. Très belles, m'sieu!*"

"*Bien. Merci beaucoup.*"

Luke turned away. He glanced back along the waterfront. Black-eyes was nowhere to be seen. Odd. From the side of his eye Luke saw a flicker of white. The man had been standing nearby, behind the trunk of an enormous flamboyant. But he had only been getting into his car, an old Citroën 2 CV. A rented car, thought Luke. Only a Frenchman would deign to own such a Citroën and the man did not look French.

Luke went to his Vespa, cranked it into action, swung out on the street. He drove past the fabled old Grand Hotel, now occupied by the French Army, then turned up to the highway and so departed town.

Once over the hill between Papeete and Faaa traffic thinned out and Luke sputtered along at a good clip. The afternoon sun was dropping upon the bizarre silhouette of Moorea. The kilometer posts fell behind. To the right, behind a fringe of cocoanut palms was the lagoon, with surf crashing soundlessly over the reef, half a mile offshore. Lagoon, reef, coral: Luke knew them well indeed, and all their inhabitants: sea urchins, cowries, *bêches de mer*; the brilliant little fish; the groupers which hid under the coral; the bizarre pipe-fish. Other creatures were less pleasant: the stone-fish, the moray eel; the *hue-hue* or puffer, deadly poisonous if carelessly cleaned and eaten; the occasional shark. The Tahitians insisted that any shark inside the lagoon was harmless. A smart slap on the surface was said to frighten them away: *"Voilà!"* (the slap on the water) *"Ils courent!"* ("They run!") Luke, nonetheless, gave the sharks right of way, and the Tahitians, so he observed, had a healthy respect for these sharks encountered beyond the reef. Luke had seen many of these: white shark, mako, hammerheads, gray nurses: and he considered them the most frightening creatures alive.

He passed Paea, its handsome white church and fine new school, the Chinese grocery, the cheerful homes of his friends M. Omer Tefaatau, and M. Philibert Tefau, the district sub-chief and brother-in-law to M. Omer... Some of Luke's fondest memories were of Tahitian parties, with endless music and song and drinking of Hinano. And the *tamure*... Ah! the *tamure*! which was to the hula as whiskey to milk... Out past Paea into Papara, through cocoanut groves; past thatched huts surrounded by papaya and banana, hibiscus, tiare, ginger, frangipani. After Papara the houses were less frequent and traffic dwindled to nothing. An old Citroën bounced along about three hundred yards behind Luke, but made no effort to overtake him... Mataiea and Papeari, where Gauguin had lived. At the Taravao peninsula Luke turned off the main highway toward Teahupoo, which seemed also to be the destination of the old Citroën. Old Citroëns were common... Luke's mind was on Brady and his invitation. He knew the *Dorado* well; five years before he had crewed aboard the boat on a trip down the coast of Mexico. Luke had never warmed to Brady; their relationship had always been cordial but never intimate. Perhaps a twinge of envy, Luke was frank to admit. Also, Brady carried his good fortune without humility, as if it were the natural consequence of cosmic law... Then there was Brady's new wife. A San Francisco friend had written, perhaps effusively: "Lia, the most delectable collection of female fluff since Deirdre. Strong men roll up their eyes, women weep; small boys point and say, 'Daddy, buy me one of those' and Daddy mutters, 'If I could afford it, I'd buy one for myself'. A love match? Maybe on Brady's side. Lia, being composed of whipped cream and sandalwood, has no soul." Luke wondered what Lia's sister was like. Beautiful girls rarely came two to a family. "Well, we shall see," said Luke.

Armand lived at the edge of Vairao District, in a strange old wooden house of two stories, built long ago by a French eccentric whose ghost yet prowled the premises. As Armand told the tale, the Frenchman had quarreled with the *tahua* Airo-Tane, the district's most respected witch-doctor. The *marae* of Airo-Tane's ancestors was situated on the Frenchman's property; Airo-Tane considered it his right to trespass. One day, in an angry effort to end the incursions, the Frenchman toppled the basalt necroliths. Airo-Tane came and looked, and quietly took himself away, to a secret grove at the head of Teahupoo Valley. The next day the Frenchman became violently ill. He foamed at the mouth, thrashed, and kicked, screaming that devils gnawed at his spine, and presently died. A few days later old Airo-Tane, as mild and affable as ever, returned to his home.

"And what of the Frenchman's ghost?" Luke asked Armand, only half-facetiously. "Does he give trouble?"

Armand made a deprecatory gesture. "Only on nights of the full moon. Not always then."

At the moment Armand was fishing, so Luke learned from the oldest of Armand's sisters. Luke decided not to wait, and again set forth along the road. Behind came an old Citroën: the same or another similar. The road deteriorated to potholes and ruts and ran close beside the edge of the cliff; the sun was low to the horizon and Luke drove with care.

There below: his private cove, his house, his dock and boat, from which he was departing, never to return! The thought was unsettling; he barred it from his mind.

He turned down the driveway, wound through a clump of *mape*, the Tahitian chestnut, then a darker patch of banana trees. He coasted to a halt, turned off the engine. Home — at least for a day or two longer. He climbed the steps to his front porch where he ruminated a moment, tugging at the obnoxious beard, which he definitely would shave off tomorrow, if he could find his razor. As for now, after making arrangements with Armand, it might be well to ride back to the Taravao isthmus for dinner at the hotel or perhaps the Restaurant Atchoun... An old Citroën returned east along the ridge of the cliff, heading toward Papeete. Luke hardly noticed. He showered, dressed in fresh clothes, started his Vespa and rode back up to the ridge. The sun was just now dipping into the water, casting a blaze all the way to the surging water at the base of the cliff. A beautiful sight, but dazzling; Luke needed his vision for the road. Ahead loomed a car — a Citroën, black against the sunset sky. The same Citroën? The driver was coming recklessly fast, hugging the wrong side of the road. Was he drunk? Luke swung wildly left. The Citroën moved likewise, struck the Vespa just under the seat, sent it bounding. For the briefest flicker of time Luke looked into the face of the man behind the wheel: a calm intent face burnished by the dying sunlight.

Before he could so much as wonder why, Luke sailed cleanly off the edge of the cliff, riding the Vespa out over the sharp rocks.

CHAPTER IV

IN THE MIDDLE OF THE AIR, alone except for the motor-scooter, Luke saw everything at once: the sunset sky, the cocoanut palms, the surf and sharp rocks below.

He and the motor-scooter started to tip forward, as if they were riding down the trajectory. Luke kicked hard at the Vespa, thrust it back toward the cliff. The impetus sent the Vespa hurtling in at the rocks and pushed Luke seaward. Luke fell into shallow water, fortuitously augmented by an incoming surge. He struck the shingle with force enough to stun him and was only feebly aware of being swept up toward the base of the cliff. But here he clung and when the surge drained back, Luke remained.

He lay collecting his wits…There was furtive movement on the rocks above. Luke lay limp, watching through half-closed eyes. A human shape stood silhouetted on the bronze-gray sky, in a pose consciously or unconsciously dramatic: legs apart, shoulders back, head broodingly turned down, with eyes fixed on Luke. A new surge of water swept in, lifted Luke, carried him a foot or two forward, floated him back about the same distance. Luke let himself loll, limbs loose.

The dark shape remained watching for another minute, then departed. Luke waited. Over the sound of the surf he heard the vibration of an engine, a transmission in low gear.

The Citroën had departed.

Luke waited five minutes, then crawled up the shore to a broken cocoanut bole, where he seated himself, hunched and shuddering. He tested his limbs. There seemed to be no broken bones, no serious sprains. Impact with the water and the bottom had dealt him a tremendous blow, enough to daze him, and even now there was a ringing in his ears. He felt as if he might like to vomit…Luke drew a deep breath. No point feeling sorry for himself. He rose to his feet, staggered around the base of the cliff to the beach and plodded home. Divesting himself of his wet clothes he pondered the amazing fact that someone had tried to kill him.

Why? A question of enormous fascination. The *who*, at least, was known, or, rather, half-known.

Luke considered all the circumstances. Black-eyes had waited at the post office. This argued that Black-eyes knew only his address: the number of his post office box. So Black-eyes had sat with his newspaper until Luke came to claim his mail, then, following Luke home, had tried to kill him, and now no doubt felt certain that he had succeeded.

Imagining the look of his own corpse, Luke shuddered. The situation was weird. Luke could conceive no motivation for the act. Two other events had been coincidental: the closing down of Teahupoo project and the invitation to join the *Dorado* at Nuku Hiva. Was either event connected with the third? Absurd.

Perhaps the attempted murder was no more than a ridiculous accident: an Englishman holding to the wrong side of the road. Luke rejected the idea. More probably the attack stemmed from a case of mistaken identity, the renter of Box 420 or 422 being the intended victim. Again Luke shook his head. Black-eyes would be on his guard against so basic an error.

Luke went into his kitchen, poured rum and canned guava juice into a glass and watched dusk settle over the ocean. Presently Luke became angry, more angry than he had ever been in his life. He poured more rum and decided that money must be the root of the affair: Royce money. But why attack Luke, whose connection with the estate was remote? It would be instructive to discuss the matter with Brady, and learn his opinions. More definitely than ever Luke resolved to be aboard the *Rahiria* on Tuesday.

Meanwhile, he would have a reckoning with Black-eyes. If he could find him.

Chapter V

Aboard the *Dorado* the course was southeast 136° on the gyrocompass, with the last of the northeast trades on the port beam; a course which, extended, struck the coast of South America somewhere near Valparaiso. Lia innocently inquired why they did not sail directly to their destination instead of zig-zagging here and there across the ocean; before she could change her mind Brady brought out *Ocean Passages* and explained the wind systems of the world. "We sail east now," said Brady in conclusion, "so that when we meet the southeast trades, we can reach into Nuku Hiva instead of fighting head-winds."

Lia nodded. "That's interesting."

"Yes," said Brady, "it is. I do believe there's a Bowditch aboard; you'd probably like to look through it."

Lia glanced down the deck to where Kelsey and Jean were basking in deck-chairs. "I really would, Brady—"

One of the paid hands approached, apparently with a problem. Brady said, "Excuse me a minute," and Lia went quickly off to join Jean and Kelsey.

With all sails set the *Dorado* cut a bubbling furrow through the water. Cumulus clouds stood dreaming above the horizon but never edged in close enough to obscure the sun. Who could ask more from life? Brady demanded of himself. Never before had he been fully sentient! Lia's indisposition was a thing of the past—another source of gratification—though now and again a pensive mood came over her. Oh well, shrugged Brady: a minor matter. He professed no insight into the mysteries of womanhood. Male and Female were as incommensurable as cats and crows; Lia's quirks only corroborated this point of view. She probably wasn't accustomed to idleness and needed something to do. A good job to teach her navigation: make her a true sea-going Royce!

By and large the cruise was a success. Carson as usual had been something of a trial: a situation now rectified, and Brady gave a grim chuckle. In Honolulu, the night before departure, Carson had gone off wenching. At sailing time, with Carson nowhere in evidence, Brady had slung his bag to the dock and put to sea, leaving Carson marooned. No one seemed to miss him.

Malcolm and Dorothy McClure who owned a boat of their own were in their element and vigorously savored each instant. Kelsey's attitude was more complicated: no surprise, since she was far more complicated than her father and mother, a situation comparable to the evolution of a Corvette convertible from a pair of pre-war Buicks. Kelsey was dark, vivacious, on the smallish side, with an inexhaustible capacity for mischief. Brady considered her an unpredictable little minx and was careful to maintain absolutely correct relations. With nothing better to do, Kelsey teased and agonized Don Peppergold, a pugnacious crew-cut young man with a homely bull-terrier face. But the more he excited himself, the more haughty and flip she became, while Jean Wintersea looked on from the side, trying to calculate Kelsey's technique. When Jean managed to isolate Don and engage him in small talk, he became orderly and polite.

Brady discussed the situation with Lia. "I suppose I should have evened the party out more carefully. I'd planned on Carson, of course — although Jean isn't exactly Carson's type." Especially, Brady reflected, with Carson's father married to Jean's younger sister.

Lia had a trick of listening with eyebrows raised and eyes widened, as if in a state of intense concentration. She now agreed with Brady's analysis. "Jean has never been terribly interested in men. I suppose what with her music she's never had the time. Perhaps," she mused art-lessly, "I should have studied harder at the piano myself."

Brady could not decide what she meant and the whole subject was dropped.

The *Dorado* proceeded into the southeast, through glorious blue and gold weather. During the late morning and early afternoon Brady, Malcolm McClure and Don Peppergold each stood a two-hour wheel-watch, relieving the paid hands, although with gyro-steering there was little to do except glance from time to time at the compass, occasionally trim or free a sheet. Brady navigated with assistance from and much boisterous argument with Malcolm McClure, who considered himself a navigational genius. McClure usually made the evening fix, using the 'McClure Calculated Zenith Principle'.

"Absolutely barbarous!" scoffed Brady. "Only a person predisposed against order and justice could contrive such a boondoggle!"

"Not at all, not at all!" exclaimed McClure. "To the contrary, I've organized chaos."

"You expect me to believe that? What could be simpler than shooting three stars, then — after a few trivial calculations, of course — laying down the position?"

"My system. It's simpler by far."

"Please, Mal! This isn't a cocktail party. You're talking to a man of the sea."

"I've noticed the barnacles between your ears. My system is utterly logical. Imagine the celestial surface and the earth as concentric globes. It's clear, is it not, that fixing the globes at any two points establishes their relationship? This is the basis of the system. Two star altitudes relate one sphere to the other. Calculation gives me the declination of the zenith, and with a time correction, the right ascension. I transpose coordinates to latitude and longitude and there we are. What could be simpler? I don't even need to draw lines of position. I put a dot on the chart and say: 'Right here!'"

"Unconvincing. Very very questionable. In fact, it sounds like the old Lamont system which is not only tedious but —"

"No, no, no!" The muscles in McClure's gaunt face twitched in indignation. "I can work the whole routine on a spherical trig slide-rule."

"Thereby introducing a new source of error."

"Okay," said McClure. "That's it." He slapped his palm upon the roof of the after dog-house. "We'll do this. Lia can be judge and timekeeper."

"Oh heavens," said Lia half-laughing, "don't involve me! I don't even know what you're talking about."

"You can read a watch, can't you?" Brady asked, with just a trace of tartness in his voice.

"Oh yes, if that's all you want me to do."

"That's all," said McClure. "You say: 'Get ready — get set — go.' Then Brady, you shoot your stars and plot your position; I'll shoot my stars and plot my position. We'll see who lays down a point first, then we'll recheck and see which of us is forty miles off."

"I'm too old for antics like that," Brady declared bluffly. "Too old and too smart. A pity Carson isn't here. He'd be a good match for you. As a matter of fact, Carson is a pretty fair navigator," Brady told Lia. "I've taught him quite a bit. I'll start with you too. Something everyone should know: celestial navigation."

"Oh Brady. I'd be impossible. Things with knobs and scales just confuse me."

"You'll catch on, don't worry. Mal, why don't you sit in and maybe pick up a few shortcuts?"

"Shortcuts? What's faster than no time at all?"

"How do you propose to fix a position in no time at all? I admit I'd like to learn."

"I'm designing a computer to perform all the horse-work instantly: the McClure Navigator."

"There's been a dozen of them," said Brady. "None were practical."

"None made use of modern electronics," stated McClure. "That's the difference. Nowadays with loran and consolan and satellites, the emphasis is away from a purely navigational computer. Mine would fill a need."

Lia had been thinking: Jean is a musician, Kelsey is a vamp. I'll learn navigation and show them all. She asked brightly: "How does it work?"

"It's a big wooden box," Brady told her. "Inside sits a navigator with a sextant, a chronometer, a nautical almanac. Mal punches a button, the navigator writes the position on a slip of paper and pushes it out a slot."

McClure nodded with placid good humor. "Something like that. Only the box is nine inches on the side, with three controls: an on-off switch, a selector for any of fifty major stars, an adjustment to correct for height above horizon. There are three read-out windows. The first is a clock, indicating the exact time — the instrument hears the time-tick and makes its own correction. The other two windows show longitude and latitude."

"Oh?" sneered Brady. "And how do you use this miraculous device?"

"Simple. You select a star, say Arcturus."

Lia interposed a question. "But how can you tell one star from another? This is something which has always puzzled me."

"You learn the constellations," said Brady. "It's just like learning the streets of a city."

"But they all look alike!"

"It's just a matter of familiarity," said Brady. "You'll soon learn to recognize them."

"Or else," murmured Kelsey, lounging in a deck-chair twenty feet away.

"Well then," said McClure, "back to my miraculous device. Looking through a sighting device you bring Arcturus into the field of vision. That's all — no cross-hairs, no bubble, no finagling, no nothing. The instrument automatically centers itself on the star, once the star is brought into the circle of sensitivity. The instrument includes an artificial horizon, and can be used at any time of day or night. The artificial horizon is a mirror floating in mercury, with a pendant gyroscope."

"That kind of set-up isn't practical," stated Brady. "It's been tried."

"No one has ever damped the surface electrostatically, using the earth's magnetic field as a stable reference. I won't go into the electronics of the thing. So: you turn the optics in the general direction of Arcturus, press a button. Then you do the same with another star, say Vega. Instantly your fix appears in the read-out windows. Any questions?"

"No questions," said Brady. "If the Ouija board works, anything will work."

"Don't pay any attention to Brady," Lia told McClure. "He only wants to get you excited."

"I realize this," said McClure. "Too bad, Brady. I'm not the excitable type."

Jean, also sitting nearby in a deck-chair, gave a brittle laugh. "I'm not either, luckily for Brady. Last night he asked me to play the harmonica."

"You should have brought your flute," declared Brady. "Mal dances a mean horn-pipe."

"At high school Lia used to tap dance," said Kelsey McClure.

"Kelsey!" protested Lia. "You're telling all my secrets!"

"Not all of them," said Kelsey, with a wicked grin. "But don't worry, I won't."

Dorothy McClure had been listening with half-closed eyes. She was pert and wholesome, with a clever straightforward face, curly reddish-gray hair, a complexion ruined by overmuch exposure to the sun. Now she opened her eyes and sat up. "Time goes by so fast! I remember that little skit so well; it seems only yesterday."

"What little skit?" asked Brady.

"When Lia did that tap-dance routine."

"Oh please, Dorothy! don't bring that up. I was so clumsy."

"You were nothing of the sort. Who was the other girl? Inez something or other."

"Inez Gallegos," said Kelsey. "She's dead."

"Dead? How could she be? Was it an accident?"

"She might have been accidentally murdered."

"But how shocking! I met her downtown just a few months ago; she was with a young man. She didn't introduce him, so it wouldn't have been her husband."

"She never married," said Kelsey.

"Of course she did!" Lia declared. "I'm sure she was married."

Kelsey shrugged. "If she had a husband the police couldn't locate him."

"Maybe for professional reasons she wanted to keep her marriage secret," suggested Jean.

Having no share in the conversation Don Peppergold became impatient. "Secrets, secrets!" he sang out. "Everybody has secrets."

Lia sighed. "I wish someone would tell me Brady's secrets. Does anyone know?"

"Yes indeed," said Brady. "There's two of us. God is one, I'm the other. We're both keeping quiet."

McClure said in a tone of mild complaint: "If you or your colleague would ordain a few hatfuls of wind we might log a decent daily run for a change. The current's taking us west faster than we can sail east."

"Are you in a hurry?" Brady demanded.

Dorothy McClure gave Brady an affectionate pat on the knee. "Of course not. I hope we *never* get home. I feel like I'm on a honeymoon myself."

"Life in the old dog yet, eh?" said Brady, with an appraising glance toward McClure.

The voyage proceeded. The ocean was an unbelievable bright blue, the swells were long and lazy: great low dunes of water ruffled by cat's-paws.

On the morning of June 10 a succession of rain-squalls appeared from nowhere. Gusts of wind caused the *Dorado* first to heel, then to skirl away to the west, to the annoyance of Brady and Malcolm Mc-Clure, who were more than ever anxious for easting. On the same evening a spectacular thunderstorm moved in from the northwest. Great leaden clouds burnt purple when the lightning flashed. The sound of the thunder was almost inaudible and presently the storm moved to the northeast. By ten o'clock only dancing wires of lightning could be seen which by midnight had glimmered away completely.

CHAPTER VI

LUKE DRAINED HIS GLASS, set it down with a thud. He went into the house, packed a suitcase, threw it into the old Fiat pickup which seemed to belong to Armand. He drove up to the highway and turned left toward Papeete. Parked at the spot where he went over the edge was the black Peugeot sedan of the Taravao Gendarmerie.

Luke stopped, slowly alighted from the pickup. At the foot of the cliff a pair of gendarmes were turning flashlights this way and that across the rocks... Luke pulled at his beard. How had they learned of the accident so quickly? Only one other person besides himself had known... Luke returned to the Fiat, drove on.

Along the Papeete waterfront were a number of inexpensive hotels rarely if ever patronized by tourists. One of these, a few doors from the Vaima, was the Hôtel du Sud. For 200 francs Luke rented a second-floor room with a private verandah overlooking the waterfront: a vantage remarkably picturesque.

At the Vaima he bought a ham sandwich which he took up to his verandah. Here he sat until midnight formulating and rejecting schemes and plans. The gendarmes? He could put forward no evidence other than an identification made in a tenth of a second with the setting sun in his eyes. A waste of time. Finally he went to bed and presently fell asleep.

In the morning Luke borrowed a pair of scissors from the manageress of the hotel. He slashed off his beard, then shaved with the razor he had found in his suitcase. He scowled at the strange naked face in the mirror: how ingenuous, how foolishly cheerful he looked, even while scowling! Partly responsible was his unruly overlong hair. He needed a haircut. Without halting even for breakfast, Luke went to the barber shop off Rue Général de Gaulle and there was shorn. Returning to the waterfront he bought a copy of the local newspaper, took an outside table at the Vaima and ordered breakfast ... An item caught his attention. The headline, translated from French, read: *American Scientist Suffers Fatal Disaster*. It appeared that M. Luke Royce, engaged in oceanographic research near Teahupoo, had been killed when his motorbike skidded from the road and plunged into the sea. The gendarmes, notified of the accident by a horrified passerby, had rushed to the scene but to no avail. The body undoubtedly had been swept out through the reef, the current running with great force at the time.

Luke sat brooding. The gendarmes would be disturbed if Luke did not report himself alive. Still, he need not have seen the item in the newspaper. If Black-eyes considered him dead, herein lay some small advantage for Luke ... The object of Luke's reflections came sauntering along the sidewalk: Black-eyes himself. Today with his white shorts he wore a black polo shirt, black socks and sandals.

Luke raised the newspaper across his face. The man took a seat about twenty feet distant, facing toward the harbor. Luke lowered the newspaper, studied the side of the sleek dark head. There he sat, comfortable and placid, with no pang whatever for the condition of poor Luke Royce. The next step, thought Luke, was to engage the man at closer quarters, to learn his identity, hopefully to bring him to grief.

Kill him? Why not?

Luke's stomach gave a small jerk of distaste.

In spite of haircut and shave Luke felt vulnerable. A few steps away, where Rue Bréa entered Quai Bir Hakeim, was a souvenir shop. Luke went in, bought a green and black Tahitian shirt, a pair of dark glasses, a jaunty coco-fiber hat. He looked in a mirror. The transformation was complete. He had changed to where he no longer could recognize himself.

Luke returned to the Vaima. He stopped short in disgust. His enemy had departed.

CHAPTER VII

THE *DORADO* HAD ENTERED the doldrums. The winds had fled, leaving a glassy calm. Up and down a few slow inches eased the ocean, in near-invisible heaves. The *Dorado* floated motionless, all sails loose. Brady put out a shark-watch: two crewmen with snorkels and face-masks at bow and stern, and now his guests enjoyed a mid-ocean swim. They plunged from the rail into the transparent blue water, swam under the hull, floated on the surface, splashed and sported.

Neither Brady nor Lia joined the fun. Lia, in her bathing suit, sat somewhat self-consciously in a deck-chair; Brady rowed around the edge of the group in a dinghy. Swimming with four watery miles below gave him the shudders. Suppose he were to lose his buoyancy and sink? How dark and cold and lonely would be the four miles! On rare occasions — this was not one of them — he forced himself to join the more confident swimmers, whereupon he kept his eyes tightly closed under water, to avoid seeing the sunlit blue fading through indigo into blue-black murk.

Most of the others felt no such inhibitions. Rather enviously Brady watched them playing in the water. Don Peppergold swam two hundred yards directly north. In mid-ocean sharks were no great threat, but the creatures were notoriously unpredictable. Not impossibly some pelagic monster might come cruising past, with dire results.

Brady rowed out to where Don Peppergold loafed on his back, looking up at the sky. Brady communicated his fears. "Nothing is as wicked as a shark. If one caught you out here you'd be done. Better head back to the ship."

"Okay, skipper." Don clipped back toward the ship. Brady paused to admire the *Dorado*: the rake to the bow, the generous hull, the expanse of the white sails. An excellent thing to be Brady Royce, master of the *Dorado*! Everything was going well. Lia seemed to be enjoying herself, although Brady thought to detect occasional cryptic moods. Depression? Boredom? Hard to believe. Brady gave his head a thoughtful shake. His plans to teach Lia navigation had come to nothing, Lia showing no penchant for the subject. She held the sextant as if it were a dead animal, and turned the pages of the almanac with an air of quiet desperation. Brady felt he had no cause for complaint. Lia had tried; she clearly had done her best. Some people simply did not have navigational minds. Lia had other qualities — beauty, charm, amiability — which more than made up for her inability to lay down lines of position; in fact, if Brady had been pressed to criticize his beautiful new wife he would have specified only her baffling and sometimes irritating reticence. Perhaps she felt constrained by the presence of her sister. The two shared no obvious affection and from time to time bickered in low voices, stopping short only when someone came within earshot. Brady did not know what to make of Jean. She was attractive, even fascinating, in an odd over-civilized way. In a science-fiction movie she might, without makeup, have played the part of the Martian woman. At times Brady had to admit that she intrigued him. Lia was beautiful, but just a trifle listless. Jean, though pale and withdrawn, looked anything but listless, and seemed to be continually roiling with unorthodox impulses.

No one was perfect, reflected Brady, not even himself. He took it for granted that his guests, if only subconsciously, resented him — for his wealth, and for the authority that, as master of the *Dorado*, he exerted over them. In his turn he felt impelled to play the role: the bluff, half-benevolent, half-irascible tyrant. But he really wasn't like that at all. Brady gave a despondent grunt. There were worse things than being poor; at least you knew who your friends were. When you married a beautiful young wife, you knew for sure what she thought of you, and everyone else knew for sure too.

Brady gave a grim chuckle. If he were poor, with no wealth, no *Dorado*, no Golconda, he might have no friends and no beautiful young wife either. Best to accept things as they were. Who the hell cared what people thought in the first place? Be damned to everybody!

Brady rowed back to the *Dorado*. Lia, Jean and Kelsey McClure stood together on the deck. Lia's bathing suit was old rose, Jean's was white, Kelsey's was baby blue. A highly palatable picture, thought Brady. Lia of course was the most beautiful. Jean was more intense and, well, yes, more intelligent. She was not so supple, so well filled-out as Lia; she was built like a fashion model, though she probably would have resented the comparison. Kelsey was smaller than either of them, with a slender energetic body. Kelsey also was a rather puzzling young woman. Watching her toy with Don Peppergold, Brady wondered if she might not have something of a malicious streak. Lia displayed only a vague absent-minded vanity that offended not even other women. Jean seemed unaware of her own peculiar appeal. Kelsey was aware of everything. She knew how men felt; she knew how to make them feel even more so. Brady had heard rumors that during her adolescence she had been something of a problem.

The swimmers all climbed back aboard the ship; Brady and the shark-watch followed; the dinghy was hoisted aboard. William Sarvis, Chief Engineer aboard the *Dorado III* and now the *Dorado IV*, came to consult Brady. "We won't have more wind today. Might be a good idea to give the diesels a spin. They could stand a bit of exercise."

Brady considered the sky. It was blank of clouds except for a few nubbins of cumulus far over the eastern horizon. He gave a curt nod. "Start 'em up."

Sarvis turned away. The engines coughed, the exhaust gargled and bubbled. Five minutes later that spot where the ship had paused, where the passengers had swum, was a half-mile astern, indistinguishable from any other spot on the face of the ocean.

CHAPTER VIII

LUKE CONSIDERED HIMSELF the most reasonable and tolerant man alive. But here was a special situation. It was bitter frustration to find that his quarry had taken cover. "Still," Luke told himself, in order to put his emotion on a rational basis, "no one has ever tried to kill me before."

He searched north and south along the waterfront. Black-eyes might have sauntered off in any of four or five directions. Where, on this placid Sunday morning, would so restless a man be apt to go? To his hotel? To the rented Citroën, for a ride in the country? To church? Not bloody likely.

Luke walked to the Quai du Commerce, examined the decks of the *Godesund*, a Swedish cruise ship tied up to the wharf. No sign of his enemy.

Luke returned along the waterfront, beside the moored yachts, past the *Rahiria*, searching in all directions. Black-eyes was nowhere to be seen. Luke crossed to the Vaima, flung himself into a chair and prepared to wait. Sooner or later Black-eyes must return along the Quai Bir Hakeim, and so come into his range of vision.

Luke waited two hours, drinking coffee, while the folk of the town passed along the sidewalk. A large group from the Swedish cruise ship appeared, walking in a stately herd. All were dewed with perspiration; all appeared vaguely uneasy as if they felt inadequate to the legends. Some were glum, some muttered and nudged each other, some contrived a thin gayety. It was difficult to be a Swede, reflected Luke.

Time passed. Luke looked at his watch. Two o'clock. Black-eyes undoubtedly had returned to his hotel for lunch, and now sat out on the terrace with a tall rum punch. Luke called a cab. He visited each of the large hotels in turn, looking through lobby, bar and terrace, scrutinizing those who lay on the beaches. He dared not inquire at the desks; the clerks might mention him to Black-eyes. Everywhere the result was negative. Luke returned through the lavender dusk to the Vaima. Here he himself drank a couple of rum punches.

The events of the previous evening began to recede. They were too grotesque for credibility. Luke blinked and shook his head. Without a focus, his first rapture of rage was hard to maintain. Luke began to reason with himself. Might the episode simply be coincidence? An ordinary run-of-the-mill accident? Luke grimaced. This was carrying dispassionate analysis too far. The circumstances were all too real. The bruises along Luke's ribs ached with a real ache. Once again Luke became angry. So then, what of the future? Assuming that he had not located, identified and punished Black-eyes by Tuesday, as seemed more than likely, should he sail aboard the *Rahiria* anyway? Or should he remain in Papeete? Luke inclined first one way, then the other. Meanwhile lights appeared up and down the waterfront. Quinn's, a block up the street, showed its ancient festoon of olive-green bulbs.

At eight o'clock Luke gave up his vigil. At the Chez Chapiteau on the Rue des Ecoles he dined on steak, *pommes frites*, a bottle of claret. Returning to the waterfront, he passed Quinn's, and for lack of better entertainment, looked in through the open doors. The orchestra: three guitars, drums, a string bass, saxophone, was rendering *Rose of San Antone*, with Polynesian whoops and hoots. The cavernous interior was already crowded. The dance-floor pulsed to the vehemence of the dancers, two-thirds of which were Tahitians wearing garlands of flowers, totally indifferent to the fact that a hundred ladies and gentlemen from the Swedish cruise ship, sitting at an isolated section of tables reserved for them, had traveled half-way around the world to inspect them. French soldiers, sailors, a contingent of Foreign Legionnaires in white undress caps, stood at the bar or danced with the girls: the notorious, somewhat unkempt and completely unrestrained 'Quinn's Girls'.

Elsewhere, crowded in booths, knee to knee around tables, were tourists from the hotels, sun-burned young men from the yachts, Frenchmen and Frenchwomen in garish clothes from the holiday camp

on Moorea. There was too much color, too much din, too much movement to be encompassed. The Swedes in particular seemed dazed.
Pushing to the bar, Luke fortuitously found a vacant stool and ordered
a bottle of beer. Immediately he saw the man whom he had been seeking all afternoon. Black-eyes sat at a table near the wall with a young
Tahitian woman in a very tight red and blue pareu. On her head, somewhat askew, was a crown of ginger blossoms. Tonight Black-eyes wore
gray slacks, white shoes, a light-weight turtle-neck shirt striped black,
grey and white. A rather vulgar outfit, thought Luke with a trace of dis-
appointment. He would have preferred a gentleman for his murderer.
Black-eyes was something of a puzzle. He had the arrogance of a lord;
he was undoubtedly handsome, if speciously so; he looked deft and
competent. A professional killer? Luke's spine tingled. He watched
in fascination. Black-eyes sat back in a relaxation close to boredom, a
long thin cigar smouldering in his fingers. The girl performed her most
trusted exertions: pouting, hunching her shoulders, wrinkling her pug
nose, tilting the ginger lei even more precariously over her forehead.
Black-eyes watched in noncommittal amusement. The girl was not
altogether to his taste, and Luke would have agreed that she looked
blowsy and well-used, at the dangerous verge of portliness.

The music came to a thudding halt, like a stampede stopping short
at the edge of a cliff. The musicians stood back to catch their breath,
the dancers moved off the floor. Voices, laughter, the clink of glass-
ware were suddenly audible. Only temporarily. The musicians shifted
position, the guitarists stepping forward, the saxophonist taking up a
baritone ukulele, the drummer tucking a leather-topped drum between
his knees. A pause, an expectancy: then four quiet chords on the
ukulele; four quick chords from the guitars: the *tamure!* Ignoring all
protests, the girl pulled Black-eyes out on the dance-floor. Luke craned
his neck, but they were lost in the seethe.

Luke turned his glass this way and that, watching the lights twinkle
and distort around the islands of foam. He had found Black-eyes: what
now? Luke had no clear idea. It occurred to him that he had failed to
define his objectives. What did he want to do?

Most urgently Luke wanted to know *why*, so he decided. Revenge,
legal or otherwise, could follow. Investigation therefore was in order.

Luke leaned back against the bar, watching the dancers convulse, writhe and jerk. The music halted. The dancers gave a great sigh, then shuffled from the dance-floor. Twisting in his seat Luke fleetingly met the gaze of Black-eyes, but let his eyes slide past. When he looked back Black-eyes was signaling the waitress. Evidently he intended no immediate departure.

A second girl came to sit at his table: a friend of the woman in the red and blue pareu. The newcomer was younger and more supple, with a fresh smiling face. Black-eyes sat up straighter in his chair. The woman in red and blue scowled across the dance-floor.

Luke thoughtfully drank the last of his beer. The music began once more: an old island tune derived perhaps from a missionary hymn. Luke gave a sigh for his easy old life; the time had come when he must commit himself. He stepped down from the bar stool, gave his shoulders a shake, crossed the room to Black-eyes' table, halted in front of the girl in the red and blue pareu. *"Voulez-vous danser?"*

She looked up, gave Luke a dispassionate scrutiny. Then, glancing toward Black-eyes and the girl who had just joined the table, she shrugged. *"Oui, m'sieu."*

Luke steered her across the floor, shuffling dispiritedly to the music. The girl smelled of ginger blossom, perfume, sweat; her body felt bulky; her hair rasped against his cheek.

Presently she pushed slightly back, to look up with a gap-toothed grin. "You American, *oui?*"

"Right," said Luke. *"Et vous?* What about you?"

"Moi? j'suis Tahitienne!" And she gave Luke a look of amused wonder. "You like Papeete? Nice place, eh?"

"Very nice indeed."

"That's good. Lots of pretty *vahines*. Where you stay?"

"I'm at the Blue Lagoon," lied Luke.

"Nice place. *Très cher.* Costs too much money, eh?"

"Right. Far too much."

"You like pretty *vahine* for girl friend? Maybe you like take nice girl back to States?"

"I'm afraid that's out of the question. By the way, that man over there at the table: what is his name?"

The girl gave a complicated shrug and grimace. She tugged at Luke's arm. "Come on, we sit down; you not a very good dancer. But you buy me a drink."

"With pleasure."

They returned to the table. The girl dropped into her seat and Luke, pulling up a chair, essayed a friendly grin toward Black-eyes. "Mind if I join the group?"

"Help yourself."

"I'm Jim Harrison." And Luke smiled expectantly toward Black-eyes.

"How-de-do." Luke was favored with a glance so cursory as to be insulting. Then prompted perhaps by a sudden subconscious admonition Black-eyes looked back with a glitter of puzzled interest.

Luke hastily signaled the waitress. "What's everybody drinking? Rum punches for the girls? What's yours? Er, what's your name?"

"Scotch and soda."

"A bottle of beer for me." Luke turned once more to Black-eyes, considering subjects which might make acceptable small talk. As he thought, there was a shuffle and bump and someone else joined the group: a massive heavy-shouldered woman with a slab-sided face, a wild bush of coarse black hair under a palm-frond hat, a festoon of *pikake*. She gave Luke an enormous grin, squeezed herself and a chair up to the table.

"*Voilà Odette,*" said the girl with whom Luke had danced, in a subdued voice.

"*Bonsoir, tout le monde!*" called Odette in a hoarse voice. She nudged Luke with her elbow. "What you think, cowboy? How you like?"

"Everything is fine," said Luke. "Odette, let me introduce you to —" he looked toward Black-eyes. "Sorry, I didn't catch your name?"

"Ben Easley."

"Odette, meet Ben Easley."

"How-de-do."

"Hi, cowboy." Odette pushed closer to the table, appraised the bottles and glasses. She spoke in Tahitian to the other girls, provoking them to mirth.

"What in the world are they saying?" inquired Ben Easley, mildly curious, addressing no one in particular.

"They're dividing us up," said Luke. "That's my guess."

Easley raised his glass. "I hope the big one likes you."

"She's a formidable woman," Luke agreed. "Your first time at Quinn's?"

"Yeah."

"You can't have been in Papeete very long."

"Not too long."

Straining to maintain his amiable grin, Luke said, "I've been around a couple of months. Long enough, actually. Time to move on."

"Two months? You must be loaded. It costs a fortune to live here." Easley had a characteristic mode of speech, a clipped sardonic rasp.

"Too right," said Luke. "I cut every corner I can. Where are you staying?"

"Big place up the road." Easley glanced across the table toward Odette and her two friends. "The local population isn't all it's cracked up to be. Where are the dollies in cellophane skirts?"

"Here, there, around the island. They exist."

"You know some of them?" For the first time Easley regarded Luke with interest.

"A few."

"What are they like? Real friendly?"

Luke pursed his lips. "About like girls everywhere, I'd say — maybe just a little bit more so."

Easley leaned back in his chair and lit a new cigar. Odette put her elbows on the table, looked from Easley to Luke, back to Easley, each movement wafting an opulent odor of rose talcum powder toward Luke. "One of you fellows going to buy me a drink?"

"Not me," murmured Easley.

Odette swung around upon Luke. "Hey, cowboy, buy me a drink, eh?"

"Oh well," said Luke uneasily, "why not?" He signaled the waitress.

"You pretty good guy. That guy —" Odette jerked her thumb toward Easley "— he cheap *popaa*."

Easley paid no heed.

Odette shoved Luke with her elbow. "You know me? Odette."

"Yes, we've met," said Luke.

"That one's Aiinea, that one's Ellie. She's my daughter." Ellie, the pretty one, grinned: a wide, bashful, rather appealing grin. "Eh? What you say?" bellowed Odette. "I'm pretty good mama, eh? I drink, you drink. You got *popaa*, I got *popaa*."

"Is she saying 'papa'?" Easley asked, mildly curious.

"No," said Luke. "*Popaa* is 'white man'. Sounds like she's hinting for a double date. She's interested in you, I believe."

"I'm not her type," said Easley.

The music started. Easley quickly rose to his feet, walked around the table to Ellie, led her out on the dance-floor. Odette and Aiinea examined Luke, but he pretended not to notice.

Quinn's had filled to capacity. Faces flickered and glimmered among the lights and colored shadows; the music was secondary to laughter, whoops, shouted conversation. In one corner a fight started; with a dexterity approaching elegance a pair of bouncers flung the combatants into the street.

The music halted; Easley returned to the table, his arm around Ellie's waist. He called the waitress and ordered for himself and Ellie. Odette and Aiinea watched with undisguised disgust; but now they were distracted by a pair of lurching young Foreign Legionnaires.

Assuming his genial grin, Luke called down the table to Easley: "Do you plan to stay in Papeete long?"

The persistent affability at last appeared to arouse Easley's suspicion; he pierced Luke with a black-eyed stare. "What?"

Luke was sure he had heard. With the smile fixed and stiff on his lips, he repeated the question.

Easley's suspicion, if such it was, passed. "Not too long," he said gruffly. "I'm leaving Tuesday, going out to the boondocks."

Luke's grin slowly became unfastened; his jaw dropped. " 'Boondocks'? The outer islands? Aboard the *Rahiria*?"

"Yeah."

"That's a coincidence. I'm going out on the *Rahiria* myself. At least I think I'm going on the *Rahiria*," Luke said in a thoughtful voice. The old schooner might be somewhat small should Easley discover his identity. And why should Easley be sailing on the *Rahiria* in the first place? Like Luke, to meet the *Dorado*? Luke's mind reeled. He shook his head in despairing perplexity. So many variables, so many imponderables!

Easley had noted Luke's bewilderment, and Luke felt the chill of the black eyes. But now Easley was diverted. A Foreign Legionnaire approached the table, to lean over Ellie. Easley lifted his eyebrows in disapproval. The Foreign Legionnaire, a blond German with a fine yellow mustache, paid no heed. The music started. Easley rose purposefully but before he could act the German had hoisted the girl and with a brisk Teutonic gesticulation swept her out on the dance-floor.

Easley returned to his seat, to sit staring into his drink. Luke watched with eery fascination. This might be Easley planning his own murder. Luke winced. Perhaps it was time to be leaving. He had achieved his minimum objectives. The man's name was Ben Easley; on Tuesday he would be sailing aboard the *Rahiria*. But Luke's stubborn streak objected. What was the quotation about alcohol and a loose tongue? *In vino veritas?* If he poured enough liquor into Easley he might learn something more. There was the equal possibility of disaster. He could hardly pour liquor into Easley without taking a drink himself; the evening might end with the two babbling their secrets into each other's ears...Luke saw something which stiffened him in his seat: his cousin Carson, somewhat drunk.

CHAPTER IX

CARSON SAT HALF-SLOUCHED, an elbow on the bar. He had not yet seen Luke through the dim lights and surging shadows. Additionally Carson did not seem particularly alert. Through Luke's mind flickered a terrible conjecture, that Carson and Ben Easley were associates, together planning his death... Insane!

Another possibility: suppose Carson saw him and bawled "Hey Luke!" This would make for embarrassment. Luke half-rose to leave, then slowly settled back. Carson was not about to recognize anyone. Other questions suggested themselves. Why and how was Carson here? Surely the *Dorado* was not in port! Warily Luke studied Carson. In many ways, he was like his father — a loose, untidy, less definite and younger Brady Royce. His hair was dark and lank; he displayed Brady's heavy cheek-bones; his mouth, somewhat over-full, hung in a petulant droop. But Carson was not all bad. His wilfulness and brazen indolence were tempered by a rather charming gayety, an easy generosity.

The theory of Carson conspiring with Ben Easley was absurd. But the puzzle of Carson's presence in Papeete remained. To resolve the mystery was simplicity itself; he need only ask Carson.

But first: were Easley and Carson known to each other? Luke furtively watched Easley, who could not have avoided seeing Carson, only ten yards distant, in the full illumination of the yellow lights above the bar. Easley sat brooding across the dance-floor. Easley was becoming drunk, thought Luke. His black eyes were almost wetly brilliant; he moved with studied control. He showed no interest whatever in Carson.

Spotlights shone upon a platform high against the back wall. A girl in a grass skirt appeared; she gyrated, heaved and oscillated. Easley gave her the whole of his attention. Luke arose, walked to the bar, touched Carson's shoulder. Carson gave a raucous cry. "I was looking for you!"

"Quiet," said Luke. "Come around to the other side of the bar."

"What's wrong with this side?" asked Carson. "I'm watching those calisthenics. It's like a woman with no hands trying to get out of a corset."

"Never mind that just now," said Luke, glancing toward Easley. "Come around over here."

Carson followed him around the bar. "Why all the mystery? Are you trying to dodge somebody?"

"Not exactly. What are you doing in Papeete?"

"The same thing you're doing: waiting for the *Dorado*. The old man sailed from Honolulu without my permission, in fact I wasn't even aboard. So I flew down on the credit card. Now what's all the mystery? Who are we hiding from?"

Luke pointed out Easley. "The dark-haired fellow next to the girl in red and blue. Do you know him?"

"Never saw him before in my life."

"His name is Ben Easley."

"If his name was Jesus Christ I still wouldn't know him. Does he know me?"

"Apparently not. He's a bill collector, something of the sort. I told him my name is James Harrison, so don't recognize me. Above all, don't call me 'Luke'. Got that?"

"Nothing to it. 'James Harrison', yes; 'Luke Royce', no. What else?"

"Discretion. Does Brady know you're here?"

"I talked to him by radio. I guess he knows. I don't think he cares. His wife has him hypnotized."

"Oh? What's she like?"

"Hard to say. She once had a job modeling clothes, if that answers your question. I take it you're joining the cruise?"

Luke nodded. "I'm sailing up to the Marquesas, to go aboard there."

Carson blinked, lurched, drained his glass. "When do you leave? I'll come with you."

"Tuesday. On the *Rahiria*. It's a schooner, not too comfortable. No stewards, no lap robes, no shuffleboard."

"Who cares? I'm in revolt against civilization. We're all too soft, too careful, too tidy. I plan to devote myself to the elementals. Food, drink, TV, females. If I were you, Luke —"

"Not 'Luke'! 'Jim Harrison'! Remember, you don't know me! We're strangers!"

"Luke, you amaze me!"

"I'll explain some other time. But for now — incidentally, where are you staying?"

"Hotel Tahiti, in a little thatch hut, with artificial lizards on the ceiling."

"I suspect they're real. If I were you I'd go back to the hotel. You've got a snootful."

"I know, Luke —"

"Jim Harrison!"

"Okay, okay. But this is exactly what I mean. Look at you now. Respectable, clean-cut, sober — and so ashamed that you call yourself Jim Harrison. Look at me. Drunk, raggedy-ass, but proud! I call myself Carson Royce! See the difference?"

"Yes, yes, the 'elementals'. Goodby, goodnight. Go back to your hotel. I'll see you tomorrow."

"Much too cautious, Luke. It's a pity."

"Perhaps so." Luke patted Carson on the shoulder, gave a final gesture of admonition, and returned through the press of shoulders, torsos and hips, to the table.

Easley was to the stage where even Aiinea looked good; he had committed himself to the extent of listening to her remarks and making an occasional humorous grimace. Odette had given up and taken herself elsewhere.

Luke licked his lips and once more brought forth his genial smile. "Place is getting crowded," he told Easley.

Easley agreed. "It's a madhouse. All these soldiers yet. Do they expect an invasion?"

Luke signaled the waitress, ordered Easley a double Scotch on the rocks, a bottle of Hinano beer for himself.

"I won't ask why all the largesse," said Easley. "I'd rather not know." He lifted his glass. "Cheers. Two more like this and I'll recite a poem by Longfellow."

"Cheers," said Luke. "What poem did you have in mind?"

But Easley's attention was diverted by Aiinea, who giggled and nudged him with her elbow.

Luke looked to where she pointed, to see Carson dancing a clownish contemporary jig in the company of the monstrous Odette. Luke rolled his eyes toward the ceiling, then looked at Easley, who exhibited only contemptuous amusement.

The music halted; with fiendish perversity Odette brought Carson back to the table. "Sit down, cowboy, sit down. You dance very hard, you poor tired drunk cowboy. Maybe one more drink, eh?"

"Sure. One more drink for all." Carson called the waitress. "Set 'em up!" He turned a leer of dreadful intimacy upon Luke. "What's yours, cowboy?"

"A bottle of beer," said Luke in a strained voice.

"Everybody spends their money on me," marveled Easley. "Scotch on the rocks, so long as the dream goes on."

"Rum punch," ordered Aiinea. "Scotch and coca-cola," ordered Odette.

Carson looked from face to face. He waved his finger toward Luke and Easley. "I recognize both of you. Captain Kangaroo and Batman."

"Wrong," stated Luke in a trembling voice. "Still — close enough. I think we'd all better go. This place closes at midnight. Another ten minutes."

"That's ridiculous!"

"Complain to the management."

The music started: the final *tamure* of the evening. Over the table loomed the German soldier with the handsome blond mustache. Apparently he had misplaced Ellie and was seeking a replacement. He addressed himself to Aiinea. *"Voulez-vous danser, mademoiselle?"*

Aiinea grinned and shuffled her feet. Easley glared up in outrage. "Get lost. *Heraus*, you stupid kraut."

The German raised his blond eyebrows. "You speak to me?"

Aiinea held up her hands in alarm. "You two be nice boys. Sit down, we all drink."

The German bowed stiffly. *"Alors, nous dansons; c'est mieux."* He gave Easley the briefest and most wooden of side-glances.

The German reached to assist Aiinea to her feet. Easley arose. "The lady, so it happens, is with me."

The German seemed not to hear. Easley pushed his hand away; the German shoved Easley back into his chair, which tilted backwards, toppling Easley to the floor.

Aiinea and Odette yelped in excitement; Carson gave a caw of laughter. Easley jumped to his feet. The German cuffed him smartly on the ear. Easley stood back glaring, then came forward, a creature of the utmost menace. Before he could strike, the bouncers arrived. The German assumed a posture of innocence and forbearance; Easley was seized and hustled swearing and stamping out the door.

The German gave his head a jerk of approval; glancing incuriously toward Luke, he escorted Aiinea out upon the dance-floor. Odette seized Carson and led him away; they disappeared into the crowd. Luke waited until midnight but saw no more of Carson.

The next day, calling at Hotel Tahiti, he was told that Carson was not in.

CHAPTER X

BRADY SAT IN THE SHADOW of the mainsail, pretending to doze. The afternoon was warm; the wind was capricious; overhead vast constructions of cumulus reared into the upper air.

Brady slouched with his white cap tilted over his nose, watching the game Jean Wintersea and Kelsey played with Don Peppergold. Jean had become interested in Don; Kelsey, previously lukewarm, was now stimulated to exert herself. Still, neither wanted to commit herself too openly for fear that Don should conspicuously prefer the other; hence Don was treated to a bewildering campaign of ploys and plots, enigmatic half-smiles and equally perplexing snubs. Brady looked toward Lia, where she lounged on a cushion, gazing out across the ocean. What in the world was she thinking? Now she frowned a trifle, now she gnawed at her lower lip. Brady knew that if he asked for an explanation, her only response would be a wide-eyed stare. A phrase rose unbidden into Brady's mind, from some back chamber of his subconscious: "A woman without a soul." Brady scowled, adjusted his cap, heaved himself erect. He looked at his watch, surprised to find that the time had gone so fast. In fact — He glanced at the sails, at the water, at the wake, at the sky; he performed a mental calculation. Now was as good a time as any.

He touched a button. Hector the Filipino steward appeared. Brady gave him a nod. "Now."

Hector went below and a moment later reappeared with a tray of champagne glasses and an ice-bucket with four dark green bottles.

Corks popped; Hector poured and served.

"What's the occasion?" asked Don Peppergold.

Brady pointed back the way they had come. "There's the Northern Hemisphere." He pointed ahead. "There's the Southern Hemisphere. At this instant we are crossing the equator."

CHAPTER XI

ONE O'CLOCK TUESDAY AFTERNOON, an hour before sailing time: the *Rahiria* seethed with activity.

Passengers, friends, relatives crowded the deck, passed up and down the gangplank, in a blaze of flower crowns and coronas, vivid shirts and pareus. All were excited, some were drunk. Luke came aboard, paused to get his bearings. The *Rahiria* was a hundred and ten feet long, a husky, German-built ship, devoid of brightwork, unknown to varnish, the timbers and decks scarred by forty years of weather and hard knocks.

There were two cargo hatches and two deck-houses. The hatches were situated forward of each mast, the houses aft. In the forward house were the crew's quarters and the galley; in the after house were the saloon, four small cabins for the passengers — these to port and starboard — cabins for the captain, the supercargo and the engineer. The sails were stout oatmeal-colored canvas, the hull was rusty black, the deck-houses a nondescript gray. The hatches were now burdened with deck passengers and their multitudinous belongings.

Luke approached a chubby man wearing shorts, a white and blue shirt, a dark blue nautical cap, who, at a guess, might be Polynesian mingled with Portuguese and Chinese. "Are you the supercargo?"

"*C'est ça!* That's me!"

Luke tendered his ticket; the supercargo took him to a cabin on the starboard side of the after deck-house. It contained upper and lower bunks, a pair of lockers, a low stool, a rectangle of gray carpet on the deck. Luke's room-mate sat on the lower bunk: a middle-aged Chinaman wearing a shiny black suit.

Luke and the Chinaman bowed, smiled, shook hands.

"My name," said Luke, "is Jim Harrison."

"I am Ching Piao; you call me Ching. I sleep downstairs below, okay?"

Luke understood Ching to be referring to the lower bunk. "Wherever you like."

"Good. I get seasick very much. Too bad."

"Too bad, indeed," agreed Luke. The cabin was somewhat warm. Luke pushed open a porthole, looked out upon the dock. He observed Ben Easley, sauntering toward the gangplank, a thin black cigar clenched between his teeth.

Luke's stomach muscles constricted; he felt a sudden reluctance toward going out on deck — could it be fear? Yes, it was fear. Luke smiled, amused and annoyed by his qualms. Deliberately he strode out upon the deck.

Easley, mounting the gangplank, halted at the rail, glanced casually around the deck, paying Luke the gratuitous insult of non-recognition. He spoke briefly with the supercargo and was conducted to his cabin.

Luke thought that he seemed fretful and preoccupied.

Other passengers came aboard — a middle-aged couple, in near-identical suits of cloud-grey seersucker. Both were thin as whippets, fair, with scrubbed pale pink complexions and ash-blond hair. Eyes averted, they edged through the Tahitians, mounted the gangplank: cool, humorously aloof in the manner of veteran globetrotters. They spoke to the supercargo; Luke heard the clipped consonants and plangent vowels of far-away England. With a final wry glance toward the Tahitians the two went to their cabin.

Next aboard was a man Luke knew well by sight and by reputation: a certain Rolf Clute, originally of Norway. Clute, a man of many enterprises, lived at the edge of the Mataiea district, in a *fare* of his own construction, with a Tahitian wife and half-a-dozen beautiful daughters. Luke had heard him described, without rancor, as a rascal, a beachcomber and, less precisely, a drunken Swede. Today Rolf Clute was sober and well turned-out, in suntan trousers, a white shirt stylishly half-unbuttoned, pointed red-brown shoes. Luke hoped that Clute would not recognize him; if so, the fat was in the fire.

But Rolf Clute, affable and waggish, merely gave Luke a wave of the hand, and went to chat with the supercargo, with whom he seemed to be on intimate terms. Turning from the supercargo, he called out in Tahitian to one of the deck passengers, and took his suitcase around the port side of the deck-house.

Sailing time was close at hand; never had Luke seen such a frenzy of confusion. Up and down the gangplank streamed the deck passengers, their friends and their relatives, carrying paper bags, jugs, stalks of bananas, cardboard cartons, guitars, suitcases. Two motorbikes, a wheelbarrow, a crate of live chickens were brought aboard. In spite of the supercargo's protests a pig was placed in the port life-boat. The farewells became fervent, tears fell; underfoot was a litter of empty Hinano bottles. Those departing staggered under heaps of flower leis; everyone embraced repeatedly.

A deck-hand went to stand by the gangplank; the supercargo went forward, urging all visitors ashore. In line with the genial unpredictability of everything Tahitian, the *Rahiria* was about to sail precisely on time, if not sooner. Luke searched the pier, praying that Carson had forgotten all about his plan to make the trip north. Aboard the *Rahiria* Carson could only be a source of uneasiness — though his presence might well catalyze new information in regard to Ben Easley. But, in the long run, it would be far better if Carson neglected to show up before sailing time.

Unfortunately this was not to be the case. Idling half-heartedly along the pier, dragging one foot in front of the other, came Carson.

Luke shook his head in vexation and disapproval. Carson looked a mess. His clothes were rumpled; his eyes were red-rimmed; his mouth hung in a dyspeptic droop. With a scowl for the Tahitians he slouched up the gangplank, then looked wildly around the deck as if half of a mind to debark immediately. Carson was evidently suffering the pangs of a titanic hangover.

The supercargo came forward; Carson made a sullen exposition of his purposes. The supercargo flashed a typical Tahitian gap-toothed grin, pointed to the No. 2 hatch. Carson stared in astonishment. "You must be kidding! Get me a place to sleep!"

"Cabins all gone, boy. Too bad. Sleep on deck. Maybe you catch a flying fish."

Carson turned a glare of outrage toward the hatch. Among the passengers was a girl in a black and orange pareu, innocently beautiful, who found Carson's predicament amusing, and Carson encountered her delighted grin.

Carson hesitated. He scowled, he rubbed the back of his neck, he jammed his hands in his pockets and seemed to be talking to himself. Perhaps he interpreted the grin as admiration, perhaps he was infuriated to the point of defiance. Perhaps he wanted to get on board the *Dorado*. Perhaps, conjectured Luke, he was fleeing something, or someone, in Papeete. At any rate he turned away from the gangplank.

His eyes fell on Luke. "Hey, L—" he scowled, bemused by Luke's instant gesticulations. Luke came forward. "Don't forget! The name is Jim Harrison!"

Carson's mouth sagged in disgust. "For Christ sake. Aren't you done with that nonsense?"

"Not yet. In fact—I don't suppose you'd take some excellent advice?"

"I've been ducking advice for years, my boy."

"You're coming aboard deck-class?"

"Sure. Why not?"

"First of all—rain. Lots of it."

Carson shrugged. "I'll move in with you."

"Not on your life. Don't even speculate along those lines."

"The Tahitians don't look worried—especially that cute one."

"Deck-class food isn't too good."

"So what? It's probably no good cabin-class."

"Be that as it may—my advice to you is stay here in Tahiti."

Carson gave Luke a glance of jaundiced suspicion. "What for?"

"Never mind what for."

"Forget it; I'm going. Deck-class and all."

Luke compressed his lips. He had played his cards wrong. To ensure that Carson remain in Papeete, he should have implored him to sail deck-passage aboard the *Rahiria*. "Well then: will you do me a favor?"

"Hell no."

"I'm serious. I want you to call yourself Bob Smith, something of the sort, until we get aboard the *Dorado*."

Carson stared in wonder, then asked, in the voice of one reasoning with a lunatic: "Now why should I call myself Bob Smith?"

Luke looked right and left. "I can't give you the details now. That fellow Easley tried to kill me, deliberately."

"Come, come, Luke. This is the twentieth century."

"Who says otherwise? You asked why; I'm telling you."

Carson heaved a sigh. "Easley tried to kill you. You retaliate by calling yourself Jim Harrison. It seems a subtle revenge. Perhaps I'm stupid —"

Around the deck-house came a dark shape; Luke moved hastily away, to Carson's vulgar amusement. The man was Rolf Clute, swinging and swaggering like an old-time zoot-suiter, his mop of grizzled red hair glinting proudly in the sunlight. He came to lean on the rail between Carson and Luke, and spat through his teeth down at the dock. "Well, looks like we got a good trip. Good wind, good weather. Nice."

"I hope you're right," said Carson. "I'm in no mood for emergencies."

"Don't worry!" declared Rolf Clute. "Nothing to worry about." He pointed across the dock. "See that old woman down there? That's her nephew with her; he's coming aboard. She told him, 'Go ahead, sail on *Rahiria!*' That's all I need to know. She's a witch-woman. Lives out in Papeari."

Carson's interest was stirred. "A witch-woman?"

"Yep. That big lady in the green dress, with the big fat face." The woman looked up at the *Rahiria;* Clute shouted something raffish in Tahitian; she gave him a good-natured salute.

"I get along good with her," said Clute. "She's not one of them bad witches, not unless you get in her way. Then she's pretty bad."

"How do you mean 'bad'?" asked Carson.

But Clute only grinned and shook his head. He peered sidelong at Luke. "Seems like I seen you before. Out by —"

"My name is Jim Harrison," stated Luke.

Carson snorted derisively. Luke gave him a frown.

As if struck by a sudden thought Clute ran down the gangplank, and presently returned with three huge bottles of Hinano. He snapped off the covers, handed one to Carson, one to Luke. *"Skoal."*

"*Skoal.*" Carson tilted the bottle. Bubbles vibrated up behind the sunstruck brown glass. He brought down the bottle. "Ahh!" Bubbles still rose in Rolf Clute's bottle. They continued to rise. Carson watched in respect.

Rolf Clute finally lowered the bottle. He wiped his mouth with the back of his hand, looked shrewdly from Luke to Carson. "You fellers from the States, eh? I got two daughters in the States. The guy in my cabin he's from the States too. You know him?"

"No," said Carson. "I don't know anybody. Not even 'Jim Harrison' here."

"Here he comes now." Clute beckoned to Ben Easley. "Hey, come over here. What's your name again?"

"Ben Easley."

"This is — what's your name?"

"Jim Harrison."

"I'm Carson Royce."

Easley's face twitched, then became unnaturally bland and blank. Or so it seemed to Luke. "Welcome aboard," said Easley in an offhand voice.

Luke turned away, unable to look into Easley's face. One thing was certain — or almost certain: Carson and Ben Easley had no prior acquaintance.

From below decks came the thump-thump-chuff-chuff of the diesel; a bell clanged. The supercargo bawled orders, herded the last of the visitors ashore.

On the dock the farewells became fervent. The last leis were thrown; the last bottle tilted. The captain came out on deck, a lean Frenchman with a gray complexion and an uneven gray mustache. He gave a jerk of his head; the gangplank was pulled to the dock even while the last passengers were scrambling aboard. Lines were thrown off. The *Rahiria* eased away from the dock, swung slowly out past the breakwater. Winches rattled; the sails went aloft and bellied to the breeze. The diesel gave a final roar, then quieted; the *Rahiria* heaved quietly northward through the blue swells, with Moorea astern and Tahiti bulking green and golden to the starboard.

Carson's excesses of the past few days caught up with him; he became wretchedly seasick. Clute watched with a brisk but sympathetic shake of the head. Ben Easley moved away in distaste. Presently he retired to his cabin, and Luke suspected that perhaps he too felt unsettled.

On the foredeck the guitars had been brought out. There was singing and gayety. Rolf Clute went forward and joined the fun.

So passed the bright afternoon. Tahiti became a gray blur astern and presently, toward sunset, disappeared.

Supper was served to the cabin passengers in the saloon: beef stew, rice, sliced raw onions in oil and vinegar, bread, raw red Algerian wine. The deck passengers, filing past the galley, were served on tin plates. Carson, huddled against the No. 1 hatch, ignored the meal and Luke thought better of offering him encouragement. "The experience will be good for Carson's character," Luke told himself.

At the meal Luke made the acquaintance of the two middle-aged Britishers, Derek and Fiona Orsham, and two German students who completed the passenger list. Derek and Fiona conducted wonderfully airy dialogues in clipped well-bred accents: "The salt, dear, if you please." "Oh! Sorry. Of course. Here you are!" And: "Please may I try the sauce, dear, meat's a bit heavy." "Oh! Of course! Here we come, full speed on."

The Germans spoke no English and very little French. They muttered only briefly to each other and seemed intent on finishing the meal as expeditiously as possible. Luke's cabinmate, Ching Piao, appeared only briefly, still wearing his black suit. He smiled a brief pasty grin at the others, dished himself a small bowl of rice and gravy which he took from the saloon, presumably to the cabin. Derek and Fiona were amused. "Well, really! Do our habits offend him?" "The inscrutable Orient; something we've got to adapt to." "Yes, I know; twilight of the Empire and all that."

Rolf Clute drank largely of the wine and described the marriage of his oldest daughter to a Seattle physician. Derek and Fiona gave their eyebrows brisk twitches and murmured: "Really?" and "How interesting!" Rolf Clute, not at all abashed, poured himself another glass of wine and spoke of the marriage of his second daughter to a wealthy Las Vegas real estate broker.

"How marvellous!" and "You must be very proud of your daughters!" said Derek and Fiona.

Luke took a mug of tea, excused himself and went out on deck. Carson, sitting on the hatch, looked at him accusingly. "What a fiasco! No hammocks, no bunks, no nothing! Where am I supposed to sleep?"

"I guess you just pick a spot," said Luke.

"I never thought it was going to be like this," complained Carson. "That Chinaman in your cabin, I wonder if he'd sell his berth. How much money do you have on you? I'm a bit short."

"I've got a couple hundred," said Luke. "Take it, if it'll do you any good, which I doubt."

Rolf Clute, leaning on the rail with the breeze ruffling his curly top-knot, laughed in vast amusement. "That Chinaman, you know something? He owns the boat."

Carson threw up his hands in disgust. His attention was distracted by the pretty girl he had noticed before. Instantly his condition improved. He went to sit by her and tried to talk pidgin English. The young Polynesian buck squatting nearby grunted and stalked ostentatiously forward.

Dusk drifted out of the east, the ocean became vague. Presently the moon rose, to lay a smoky yellow trail across the water. From the foredeck came the throb of guitars, the muffled chant of Polynesian voices. Luke leaned back on his elbows. The voyage would be pleasant indeed were it not for his worries and fears and perplexities.

As if to emphasize Luke's reservations, Ben Easley emerged from the deck-house, paused a moment, then seated himself at the far end of the hatch.

"Hey Luke," called Carson. "Come over here, translate for me! This young bonbon don't take me seriously."

Luke grimaced. "Er — Clute! Carson's calling you."

"Eh? Who?"

"Carson wants you to help him out with that girl," Luke explained. Easley seemed engrossed in his own thoughts.

"Not me." Clute pointed a crooked finger. "That was Leon Teofu who walked away. He's a good fighter and he's pretty mean. I don't want him mad at me."

"That's his girl friend?"

"Leon thinks so. Carson better look out."

Derek and Fiona joined the group, and the air at once was full of verbal shuttlecocks: "What an enchanting evening." "Never like this in dear old Blighty." "Oh my aunt no." "Exactly where are we, dear?" "Hard to say. A bit north of Tahiti, or so I'd reckon it."

Fiona searched the moon-silvered horizons. "Nothing in sight. Where is our first landfall?"

"Somewhere in the Tuamotus," said Derek. "Ask Mr. Clute; he's a knowing sort."

"I think we land on Kaukura first," said Rolf Clute. "Then Apataki. Then Arutua. Then Rangiroa, and that's where I leave the ship."

"Indeed?" inquired Fiona brightly. "You're not a tourist like the rest of us?"

Clute chuckled. "My touring days are over. I'm a businessman. I got property on Rangiroa. Now I go out to look."

"How nice."

"Nice when they don't steal my copra. Some people are pretty grabby. I'm taking out a boy to watch things for me." Clute leaned forward, peered up the deck. "That's him in the white shirt, playing the guitar."

Luke looked. "That's the witch-lady's nephew."

" 'Witch-lady'?" inquired Fiona. Derek asked, "Did I hear correctly?"

Rolf Clute glanced sidewise to discover if possibly the Orshams might be indulging in facetiousness. But both were entirely in earnest. "Yeah, the big fat lady in the green dress that was sitting on the gasoline can. I've known her a long time. She witched me once on Rangiroa. I told her I knew what she was doing. I told her she'd better stop or I'd cut her throat." Rolf Clute nodded in grim recollection of the event. "She stopped the curse, just like that. We get along good now. She knows I'm not scared of her. I can take care of anything along those lines."

"My word," breathed Derek, raising his eyes to the heavens. "Witches!" Fiona gave her breathless little laugh. "One travels for new experiences, and now, my dear, you've met a witch." "Not precisely met! Sheerest, most glancing contact. We're not even acquainted."

Rolf Clute said in a deprecatory tone, "She's no real strong witch. There's some on the outer islands: *tahuas* they call 'em. They get mad at a man, they lay on a real strong curse. Then the man goes to another *tahua* to take off the curse. Otherwise he dies like a mad dog."

"Poison, most likely," was Derek's opinion. "I suppose that poison is available?"

Clute snorted. "Nothing to it. In the old days they'd just cook up a dish of *hue-hue* — that's puffer fish — or they take the poison from a puffer fish and mix it into good fish. But that was just for the common people. The *tahuas* would use a curse, or send out ghosts — *tupaupaus*, they call 'em."

"'Ghosts'? Oh really now. You're joshing us."

Rolf Clute shook his head as if at knowledge too vast to communicate. He looked up toward the No. 1 hatch. "Go up there; ask for Ari'aitere or just yell 'Jono': that's his French name."

"'Jono'?" asked Fiona doubtfully. "French?"

Rolf Clute continued. "He's from one of the oldest families; ask him about the *tupaupau* that walks around behind his house. Go over to Raiatea. Some American guy built a house on the Vaitate family tomb. He's dead, his son is dead, his uncle is dead. The house is empty. Sit on the porch the night of the full moon. You'll see all the ghosts you want."

"You've seen these ghosts?"

"Sure I've seen 'em. Dozens."

"Well, well!" "I suppose we can't dispute eye-witness testimony!"

Ben Easley came across the hatch and seated himself beside Rolf Clute. "They must have had some pretty fierce times out here."

"You betcha. Nobody gets as mad as a Polynesian. Look at 'em now, laughing, singing — you'd think they was the gentlest people in the world. Wait till they get mad. Then they go crazy." Rolf Clute jerked his thumb forward to where Carson sat with the girl. "Chances are nothing will happen. Leon Teofu will sulk and go off with some other girl. Unless he sulks too hard and gets mad. Then Carson might get a beating, or maybe cut with a knife. That's the way it goes."

"Oh my," exclaimed Fiona. "Shouldn't someone warn him?"

Rolf Clute shrugged. "I'll pass him a word." He rose to his feet, stretched his wiry arms, let them flap against his hips. "He can't get in trouble tonight. Not unless he's a pretty good man, better than I give him credit for."

Rolf Clute departed for his bunk. Easley strolled forward to the bow, where he could be vaguely seen, silhouetted against the jib. Derek and Fiona Orsham yawned and rose to their feet. "Time for shut-eye." "But it *is* so lovely out here!" "Worth all the tawdry gimcrack of Papeete." "I think I could sail on like this forever." "Yes, but we mustn't be greedy. There'll be more tomorrow." "Of course. Goodnight all." "All, goodnight!"

The Orshams departed. Ben Easley strolled down the port side of the deck, passed behind the deck-house, and presumably went into his cabin. The two Germans had retired a half-hour before. Ching was nowhere to be seen. Of the cabin passengers only Luke was yet on deck. The time was perhaps eleven o'clock.

Carson came to sit on the hatch beside Luke.

"Two things I want to emphasize," said Luke. "First: you'd better lay off that girl. Her boy friend is a pretty tough customer."

"Who? Leon? Meek as a lamb. Besides, he's not her boy friend. Titi laughs at him."

" 'Titi'? Is that her name?"

"So she tells me. Why should she lie?"

"No reason whatever. How do you exchange your little love secrets?"

"She talks French. I had French in high school. Funny how fast it comes back. Never thought I'd have any use for it."

"You don't think Leon is a threat?"

"Hell no."

"Clute says he's a tough cooky and mean as sin. If I were you, I'd lay off."

"Well, you're not me. If Leon looks at me sidewise I'll lay a karate chop on him. So much for Point Number One. What's Number Two?"

"Be careful of Easley. Really careful."

"What an odd world you live in! First Leon, now Easley."

Luke spoke in a measured voice: "I'll tell you exactly what happened. You can draw your own conclusions." He described his experiences. "The next day I shaved off my beard; I became Jim Harrison. I'm naturally interested in learning the reason for all this."

Carson seemed to be impressed. "I agree that Easley is a sinister type. Still, why should he pick on me?"

"My name is Royce, your name is Royce."

"You've never seen him before?"

"Never."

"Nor I." Carson pondered a moment. "It seems remarkable that he's headed for the Marquesas along with us. Is he planning to meet the *Dorado*?"

"Your guess is as good as mine. Exactly who is aboard the *Dorado*?"

Carson's voice took on a trace of zest. "First, the old man and his child bride. Do you watch old movies on TV?"

"I don't even watch new movies."

"Lia is like Hedy Lamarr at her best: dark hair, pale skin, a mysterious expression, not quite so slinky. She's a hard woman to figure out. Still, nothing like her sister Jean, who you wouldn't believe. She plays the flute. I patted her fanny one night and I don't think she knew what I meant; she said 'Excuse me' and moved out of the way. There's another cutie aboard, more my type: a certain Kelsey McClure, who knew Lia in high school — in fact, she introduced Lia to Brady. Then there's a junior executive known as Don Peppergold, two older McClures, and that's the lot. Some people name of Crothers made the trip to Honolulu, but they're not aboard now. By and large, a clean-cut bunch. Could it be that you're just a wee bit imaginative?"

"Call me anything you like. But don't take chances until you're aboard the *Dorado*."

"Just as you say. I can't avoid being killed in my sleep, however. Speaking of sleep, fetch me a pillow and some blankets. Do you have a spare set of pajamas? I don't suppose you'd part with your mattress?"

"And sleep on the springs? Not much. Why didn't you bring aboard a bedroll?"

Carson managed a haughty stare. "Naturally I thought I could promote a cabin."

"I'll give you a blanket and maybe a pillow. Let me check and see what's available."

Luke went to his cabin. In the bottom bunk Ching snored softly. Luke pulled the blanket from his bunk but decided against the pillow. Carson would have to make do with his suitcase, or his shoes.

Chapter XII

In the morning a brisk wind ranged out of the southeast, from the empty trade-wind spaces below Easter Island. The schooner wallowed and heeled; water rushed past the hull; the old timbers creaked and squeaked and made a hundred other less definite noises. One of these, a subdued dreary moaning, was almost human in its overtones. Luke, awakened by the multifarious noises shortly after dawn, watched the disk of sunlight admitted by the porthole sliding up and down the bulkhead. He presently traced the source of the near-human moaning to Ching in the lower berth. The cabin smelled of vomit. Luke's own stomach gave a jerk. He wasted no time going out on deck to breathe fresh air and steady himself against the horizon.

The ocean raced and rolled; whitecaps fell down the face of the blue-black waves. Luke drew several deep breaths and felt better.

The deck passengers were already at their breakfasts: coffee, bread and jam. Carson gave Luke a glance of bitter reproach, as if all his discomforts were the result of Luke's neglect. Luke returned a cheerful wave and went into the saloon. Derek and Fiona Orsham were breakfasting. Rolf Clute sat opposite smoking a cigarette.

"Good morning," said Luke.

"Good morning!" "A rough good morning it is!" "So windy!"

"Just trade-winds," said Clute. "Good sailing weather. We're going about nine knots. Maybe ten."

Ben Easley came in, wearing white shorts, his white and black sport-shirt, sun-glasses. He gave the company a reserved "Good morning", poured himself a mug of coffee. Luke studied him covertly. Amazing how a single human being could generate so dark an influence! Luke looked here and there; did the others feel the same oppression? Clute stubbed out his cigarette, raised his cup with a somewhat excessive action of arm. Derek ordered his tableware precisely in front of him. Fiona's voice became almost imperceptibly higher.

Derek rubbed his face and wondered whether he should shave. "After all, we're miles at sea." "Derek, you mustn't go slack. What would you think if I came to the table in a ghastly great bush?"

"Quite right, dear — but ladies aren't gentlemen. And, as the French say, '*Vive la différence!*' My feelings exactly."

"Beards are really so vulgar," said Fiona. "I simply can't imagine any of you wearing a beard." She looked from face to face. Luke excused himself and left the saloon. He went to his cabin, found his razor and shaved with care.

He came out and sat on the hatch. Carson joined him. "Speaking of Easley — have you done any investigating?"

Luke raised his eyebrows. "Such as what?"

"Oh — just general detective work."

"I don't know what you mean. Whatever it is — I haven't done any."

"Seems as if that would be the first order of business."

"Maybe so — but what should I do?"

"Search his luggage."

Luke grunted. "You make it sound so easy. Any other ideas?"

"Well — you might tell him you're Luke Royce. Confront him with the facts. Watch his reactions."

"Hmm. Then what?"

Carson shrugged. "It's a start. You asked for some ideas."

"And those are the best you can come up with?"

"Can you do any better?" snapped Carson.

"No. Which is why I haven't tried any detective work."

During the afternoon Rolf Clute brought out a pack of cards and enticed Carson and Easley into a poker game. Luke watched for a few minutes, then went out to sit on the hatch.

Carson's recommendations, he was forced to admit, made a certain degree of sense.

Luke grimaced. He strolled to the saloon, glanced in at the game. No one heeded him. He sauntered around to the port side of the deck-house. Here he hesitated. Embarrassing to be caught rummaging through Easley's belongings! Still — nothing ventured, nothing gained. Gritting his teeth, palms sweating, Luke opened the door, stepped into the cabin.

A new leather suitcase lay under the lower bunk — obviously the property of Easley. Luke slid it forth, puzzled a moment over the clasp, raised the lid.

Clothes, shoes, shaving gear, a case containing drugs and salves. A bottle of cologne. No papers, no letters, no documents. No passport.

Luke hastily closed the suitcase, shoved it back under the bunk. He slipped out of the cabin just as Easley came around the corner of the deck-house. Easley stopped short. "Were you in my cabin?"

"Is that your cabin?" Luke stuttered. "I thought it was somebody else's. I wanted a pillow — for Carson."

"A pillow for Carson, eh?"

"Well, he came aboard without a pillow. No blankets."

"And you were helping him out. Off my bed? It's kind of strange."

"Somebody said there was extra bedding…"

Easley gave Luke a sardonic glance, stepped into his cabin.

Luke went to sit on the hatch. Carson came to join him. "Well? What did you find out?"

"Shut up," said Luke.

" 'Shut up'? What for? Didn't you go through Easley's gear?"

"He just about caught me in the act."

"Woof! What did you tell him?"

"I said I was looking for a pillow. I told him it was for you."

Carson raised his hands in horror. "Don't involve me! I'm playing all this straight."

Luke stared glumly out to sea. After a moment Carson asked: "Did you learn anything?"

"Nothing of consequence. Easley takes pills. He's got everything from aspirin to zinc oxide."

"Prescription pills?"

"I didn't check. I just saw a medicine case full of bottles."

"If you looked at the labels you might have learned his doctor's name and his home town."

"I was nervous. With good reason."

Carson gave a dour grunt. "I suggest that next time —"

" 'Next time'! What are you saying! My career as a detective has come and gone. *You* go look for pillows in Easley's cabin."

"Not me."

Up on the foredeck Titi went to lean on the rail. She glanced back toward Carson, who at once jumped to his feet. "Time for my French lesson."

"You don't show very good sense, Carson."

"If I had good sense I'd be aboard the *Dorado*. Since I'm stupid I might as well enjoy it."

Luke remained on the hatch. Easley came back around the deck-house. For a long minute he stood looking at Luke, then went into the saloon. A few minutes later Fiona came hurriedly forth. She turned a furtive glance toward Luke, went into her cabin, emerged with her big leather handbag which, with another glance toward Luke, she took with her into the saloon.

Carson, finding Titi in a bad humor, returned aft and wandered into the saloon. Presently he came forth and joined Luke on the hatch. "They're talking about personable crooks who make their living on trans-Atlantic liners."

"I'll remember this trip a long time," said Luke.

"Why are you complaining?" said Carson. "You at least have a bed."

"I also have a sick Chinaman," said Luke.

Easley sauntered from the saloon. He halted in front of Luke, a twitching half-smile on his face. Then, without words, he strolled forward, leaving Luke in a seethe of fury and frustration.

The day passed and another: hours of sunlight, cloud and wind, blue seas and flying fish; moonlight and starlight, singing and music and earnest discourse. The Orshams treated Luke with reserve. Ching occasionally appeared on deck, his face the color of old newspaper, wearing slippers, black pants and a white dress shirt. The German students after being snubbed by the Orshams held themselves aloof. Ben Easley had time for no one but Rolf Clute; hour after hour they discussed the strange and unusual. Luke eavesdropped when opportunity offered, but Easley said nothing of himself or his past. Rolf Clute described encounters with sharks, eels, eccentric tourists. He told of cannibals and missionaries, shipwrecks and lonely atolls, prescient birds and sacred trees. He commented upon the Chinese and Polynesians, Americans and French; he discussed the mad priest of Mangareva and the evil king of Hana Hana. He spoke of taboos, forbidden islands, lepers, poisons from the sea, the upoa bird whose call foretold the death of Tahitian royalty.

Ben Easley listened with deference, smoking his long thin cigars and nodding gravely.

On the morning after the third night Rolf Clute pointed ahead: "Niau."

"Where?" cried Fiona. Derek squinted. "I can't see a thing."

"Nothing to see," said Clute with his foxy grin. "We're thirty miles out. Keep watching."

Presently a blue-gray mark appeared on the northern horizon, which gradually metamorphosed through increments of solidity and detail into a beach shaded by cocoanut palms a hundred yards behind a low reef. The *Rahiria* skirted the island, with near-naked children running along the beach keeping pace. At last on the north shore a village appeared: a cluster of thatched huts, a few spindly piers running out into the water. The *Rahiria* nosed delicately close in to the reef; sails rattled down the mast; the anchor splashed into fifty feet of water so clear that every detail of the bottom was apparent. The *Rahiria* swung slowly about with the current. A motor launch put out from the village, loaded with sacks of copra, followed by a dozen outrigger canoes, each almost awash under sacks of copra fore and aft. They negotiated an almost non-existent channel through the reef, came up alongside the *Rahiria*.

Stores, supplies, crates, were brought up from the hold; the copra was heaved aboard and stowed, the supplies were transferred to the motor launch, together with a pouch of mail.

With no further ceremony sails were hoisted; the anchor raised. The *Rahiria* sheered off to sea. Niau dwindled astern.

"A very dull visit," Fiona commented sadly. "I was hoping for a feast on the beach."

"Not many people on Niau," Rolf Clute told her. "Not much copra. Ahead is Kaukura. Look, you can see it. We'll anchor in the lagoon tonight and you can go ashore. But no feast. Not any more, unless you pay for it yourself."

Kaukura, an almost imperceptible dark line between sea and sky, in due course became a chain of islets each with a top-knot of palms. In mid-afternoon the *Rahiria* gingerly negotiated a pass through the reef, and with a man at the masthead watching for coral heads crossed to the village. A dilapidated wharf thrust out from the beach. The *Rahiria* ghosted alongside; lines were thrown ashore and made fast.

The *Rahiria* would not depart until morning; the passengers were free to go ashore.

Carson drew Titi aside and spoke to her earnestly. She grinned and shook her head, and went off with her relatives.

With a glittering stare for Carson, Leon Teofu followed.

"At least she didn't act outraged," Carson told Luke. "That's a positive factor. I'll make the grade yet."

Luke gave a disgusted grunt. "How come you can't take a hint?"

"This is a free ocean. All she needs to do is say no."

"She just said it."

"The way she said it was strictly 'yes'. The girl is mad for me!"

"Leon Teofu is getting very upset."

"So what? He's just a guy that hangs around. Let's go for a swim. Hey, Clute, how are the sharks around here?"

"Go ahead, swim. No sharks in Kaukura lagoon. At Apataki, the same kind of lagoon, sharks everywhere. Nobody swims."

Fiona and Derek came briskly past, wearing white shorts, sneakers and floppy white hats. Fiona clutched her brown bag under her arm. They ignored Luke. "We're off to the beach, for shells! Mr. Clute, do come along, you're so knowledgeable!"

"No, no, not me," said Clute. "I got business ashore, with a man that does pearl-diving. He owes me money; maybe I collect in pearls."

"How marvellous!" "Hope you come up with another Black Mogul!"

The Orshams were off to the beach.

Ching went to the Chinese grocery store and disappeared into one of the dim back rooms.

The Germans tramped dutifully around the island.

Carson wandered through the village, hoping to find Titi, or someone equally agreeable.

Ben Easley went into the store, bought a package of Gauloise cigarettes, came out to the front, sat on a bench.

Rolf Clute returned along the lane which ran through the banana trees behind the store. He wore a disgruntled expression. Sitting down beside Easley he gave a voluble explanation of his difficulties. Then he made a sly sign, and ducked into the store, to emerge with a pair of beer bottles, containing an unidentifiable liquid. He gave one to Easley, who tasted, glanced speculatively at the contents, tasted again without enthusiasm.

Luke wandered aimlessly up the beach, perhaps a quarter-mile, then returned by way of the lane which ran through the village, and went to stand in the shade of a breadfruit tree near the dock. Easley and Clute still sat on the bench in front of the store. For lack of anything better to do, Luke cut open a green cocoanut and drank the milk. Surreptitiously he watched Easley. Familiarity — if contact with Easley's brooding presence could be so described — had done nothing to dissolve the macabre aura about his person.

As Luke watched, quivering in the intensity of his loathing, Ben Easley set aside his bottle and spoke to Rolf Clute: putting a proposition or perhaps making a request.

Clute assented without fervor. The two went aboard the *Rahiria*, and presently returned ashore. Clute carried a spear-gun, Easley had a towel slung over his shoulder.

They went into the grocery store and came out with a pair of face-masks and another spear-gun, either rented or borrowed. Then they set out along the road which paralleled the lagoon.

Luke watched them disappear behind a copse of mango trees. After a moment's hesitation he sauntered after them.

Two hundred yards down the road a strip of white beach sloped into the water. Luke watched from a distance as the two men prepared to swim. Easley had donned black swimming-trunks; Clute wore merely a sagging pair of jockey shorts. They waded out until the water was waist-high, adjusted their face-masks, cocked the spear-guns and began to swim.

Luke continued slowly along the road. From behind a clump of pandanus trees he surveyed the beach. Easley would hardly carry his passport into the water; it must be with his clothes, where he had left them on the bole of a fallen cocoanut tree.

Luke waited until the swimmers were well out in the lagoon, diving down among the coral heads. Then, as inconspicuously as possible, he approached the clothes. Easley and Clute were almost invisible: two small specks. Now one ducked under, now the other. Luke reached for Easley's trousers.

No wallet, no passport, no money. Luke looked in Easley's shoes. Nothing.

Odd, thought Luke. Had Easley left his papers aboard ship?

It seemed unlikely.

What would Easley do with such objects? Entrust them to the captain, or perhaps the Chinaman in the grocery store?

Again unlikely. Easley trusted no one.

Easley would hide his papers. Luke scrutinized the beach. He lifted a cocoanut frond, looked under the fallen trunk.

Nothing.

Easley's shoes had been set down very neatly, very accurately. Luke carefully moved them, felt in the sand below.

A wallet, a passport.

Luke took them back into the foliage.

He opened the passport. Ben Easley looked out at him, the eyes wide, as if angry; the mouth drooping. The name on the passport was Benjamin Eiselhardt.

The address was 2690 Cecily Street, Apartment E, San Francisco.

The passport was new, issued at San Francisco on June 10. There was a visa only for French Polynesia, granted by the French Consul at San Francisco.

Luke looked into the wallet. The name on the driver's license was Benjamin Eiselhardt, 1615 Golden Gate Avenue, San Francisco. There were no credit cards, no photographs. The money compartment contained twelve one-hundred-dollar bills, several thousand Polynesian francs. Luke reflected a moment, smiling grimly. His Vespa had been worth three hundred dollars, more or less. His hand hung for a moment over the money. Regretfully he drew it back. In all probability he would never have another chance to collect damages from Easley, or Eiselhardt — whatever the man's name — but confiscating the sum in such a fashion seemed beneath his dignity.

Luke checked the small compartments. He found several cards. The first was imprinted: Sard's Club, with the address, 69 Homan Alley, beside a black Doric column to the side. On the back was penciled a telephone number: 659-6090.

The second was imprinted: The Martinique, 619 Ellis Street, San Francisco, with a conventionalized drawing of a Latin-American couple dancing the samba.

There were three cards from modeling agencies, all with San Francisco addresses. Very likely Easley's occupation, thought Luke. He could not imagine Easley working with either his hands or his mind in any productive capacity. The only other item was a claim ticket upon the Romeo Cleaners, on Geary Street, San Francisco.

Luke whistled through his teeth. The character and background of Ben Easley, as he chose to call himself, were somewhat less vague. Still: no enlightenment, no revelations. But what could he expect?

Luke glanced across the lagoon. Rolf Clute had speared a fish; he and Easley stood on a coral head while Clute cut at it with his knife.

After a moment Clute threw the fish into the lagoon. Luke wondered what they were up to. Far down the beach he spied Derek and Fiona returning from their shell-gathering. Hastily he applied himself to the business at hand. He copied names and addresses, replaced cards in the wallet, made a final inspection of the passport, buried everything as he had found it, and returned to the *Rahiria*.

Fiona and Derek were not far behind him. They laid out their prizes on the hatch. "Nothing very much. A few lovely textiles." "Don't forget my nice little cowries!" "Naturally not, dear. Look at this one. It's an orange helmet, or so I believe."

Sometime later Rolf Clute returned, in a state of expansive good humor. He had found the man who owed him money; the two had discussed their business over a bottle. Clute looked around the deck. "Where's that guy Easley? Isn't he back yet? When I left him he was digging around the beach, looking for his stuff."

Half an hour later Easley came aboard, face like a thundercloud. He crossed the deck to confront Luke. "How come you moved my shoes?"

Luke looked up with a sinking feeling. He was too proud to lie; on the other hand... He temporized. "Why should I move your shoes?"

"For the same reason you frisked my room!"

Luke looked up into the clamped face wondering what to say. Fiona had overheard. "Did you say 'shoes'? I took them up the beach, safe and sound from the tide. Couldn't you find them?"

Easley turned slowly away. Luke drew a deep breath. "Yes, I found them," said Easley in a carefully toneless voice. "Thank you — a great deal."

CHAPTER XIII

FIVE DEGREES BELOW the equator a series of squalls time after time sent the *Dorado* reeling over on its rail. A cloud, dense and black as an ink-blot, would appear, with a scurry of white foam on the ocean below, and then the wind would be upon the boat: a howling, whooping bluster, usually with a pelt of rain. The helmsman would instantly bring the bow into the wind, while the crew dropped the flogging mainsail and reefed the foresail. After five or ten minutes the fury of wind and driving wetness would pass and the fitful airs of doldrums would return.

In five days the *Dorado* logged only two hundred miles, and this in the wrong direction: to the southwest rather than the southeast. On a single day six separate squalls came boiling across the water. Brady finally ordered all canvas down except a pair of steadying stay-sails and fired up the diesels, to the approval of gruff old Sarvis. "After all, man, you've got fifteen hundred horsepower lying idle. Folly not to get the use of it. Your guests will like it better, as well."

To which Brady made a peevish reply: "Dammit, this is a sailing vessel, not a cocktail lounge. The guests can damn well take the good with the bad. It's been all cream so far."

Sarvis shrugged and went off to start the engines, which seemed to discourage the squalls; there was but one other relatively feeble display.

Brady, now stubborn, kept the engines running through perfect weather, to make sure of gaining back his easting, although he found every minute of running under power a trial.

There were other exasperations, each trivial in itself, but combining to build up in Brady a formless dissatisfaction, and his disposition had become testy. Lia was the principal source of his irritation. He had

expected no transports of adoration from his young bride (except perhaps in his heart of hearts) and he had found none. Brady could find
no fault in what Lia did, but what she didn't do left a void which he
could neither define nor reasonably complain about. A question began
to gnaw at his mind: had he, after all, made a mistake? Not in choosing
a bride so much younger than himself, but in choosing Lia: a woman so
withdrawn as to seem a stranger.

A stranger! Brady chewed on the word. It was not too strong. After
two months of marriage he knew no more of Lia than he did on the day
he married her.

Now Jean was another case. Brady had become increasingly aware
of Jean: a girl somewhat angular, with an odd awkward grace, a face
which mirrored a hundred subtle emotions. Jean did not have Lia's
even disposition; she was now sullen, now vexed, now exhilarated, now
downright malicious. It would be less ornamental but probably more
fun being married to Jean, thought Brady.

And somehow he conceived that he had been given to understand
that she did not find him totally unattractive...The drift of Brady's
thoughts surprised him. He hauled himself up short. "Enough of this
peevishness, old man! It doesn't become you. You'll make yourself
ridiculous!"

For on a long ocean voyage no mood or trait could be concealed;
everyone else was too watchful. Unobtrusiveness became not only a
virtue but an advantage. Here Lia excelled, reflected Brady, for all her
remarkable appearance. She irritated no one, except possibly himself.
The obverse to this quality was a certain bland opacity, or, in Lia's case
(as Brady preferred to think), a dreamy distrait quality which held an
element of charm. Kelsey and Jean apparently took the uncharitable
point of view and patronized Lia in a manner which put Brady's teeth
on edge. Here must lie the reason for Lia's fits of brooding!

One afternoon, bantering with Jean, Brady worked the conversation
around to Lia. "She puzzles me! Sometimes I'm sure there's something
on her mind. Between the two of us: what's wrong? Or is it my imagination?"

Jean gave her brittle laugh. "Lia's always been moody, dear child."

"Moody about what? People aren't moody over nothing!"

"I can't imagine."

With Jean offering no enlightenment, Brady sought out Kelsey, where she sat curled like a kitten in a deck-chair. Brady came bluntly to the point. "Lia's been moping and won't tell me why. Do you know?"

Kelsey grinned. "You do ask awkward questions."

"So you know."

"I didn't say that. Anyway, even if I did know, I'd have to deny it, and I do deny it."

Brady was not in the mood for flippancy. "Suppose she had a cancer, or was going blind: you wouldn't tell me?"

Like Jean, Kelsey laughed. "No fear. Lia's healthy. If you're worried, why not ask Lia?"

"I have. She just gives me a funny look."

Don Peppergold approached. "Who wants to join the super grand spectacular landfall pool? Biggest event of the trip!"

"Not me," said Kelsey. "I don't have any money." In the competition with Jean she long ago had won. Don was her serf and now Kelsey's main concern was keeping him in his place.

"Only a dollar per pick," said Don and explained the rules of the game.

Brady sat back and watched Kelsey macerate Don's enthusiasm. Don's big problem, thought Brady, was his wholesomeness. He was by no means a fool, but he acted like a man who drank milk with his meals.

Kelsey rose to her feet. "I've got letters to write. 'Scuse me." She skipped off. Don stared slack-chinned after her.

"Adorable little cuss," said Brady kindly. "But I pity the man she marries. She'll give him a run!"

Don ran his fingers across his blond crew-cut and wandered off in search of Jean. Brady went down to the master's stateroom. He found Lia stretched out on the bed, watching reflections on the overhead.

Brady sat down beside her. "Well, sweet, what's on your mind?"

"Nothing really. I'm just lying here resting."

Brady had the tactless habit of challenging all unreasonable statements. He spoke almost explosively. " 'Resting'? For Christ sake, there's nothing to do aboard ship but rest!"

He instantly would have recalled his words, but Lia only looked at him meekly. He started to apologize, but Lia raised herself to a sitting position. "I'm sorry, Brady. I'm not really antisocial. I was just, well, thinking about things. How nice everything is, really."

Brady was touched. He patted Lia's head. "Of course, sweet. Has anyone been hurting your feelings?"

"Oh no."

"If you have troubles — of any sort — I hope you'll come to me with them."

Lia rose to her feet and went to look out the porthole. "I'm always amazed how blue the water is."

Chapter XIV

The *Rahiria* departed Kaukura at eight in the morning, when the tides were slack and the current through the pass at its least.

At noon the ship entered blue and green Apataki lagoon, and, finding no cargo, immediately moved on to Arutua, nine miles west, to anchor directly in front of the village. The transfer of goods, in four peculiar boats built of planks and corrugated roofing, proceeded slowly, and at dusk was still underway. The captain elected to remain at anchor overnight.

Dinner, more or less as usual, was rice, canned beef and fried bananas. Rolf Clute thumped a bottle of brandy down upon the saloon table. "Tomorrow we put into Rangiroa; I leave the ship."

"What a pity!" cried Fiona. "We'll miss you!"

Derek exclaimed, "We were hoping you'd be aboard the whole trip! You're so full of information!"

Rolf Clute shook his head. "Can't be done. But you'll see me again. I'll catch the *Taporo* on its way into Papeete. When you get back I'll tell my wife to fix up a real Tahitian meal like you never see in the hotels. My daughters are real good dancers; very pretty girls."

"How wonderful!" "Are you serious?"

"I'm serious!"

"We'll be sure to come!" "But you must give us your exact address."

"Just go out the highway to the store in Papeari, at fifty-two kilometers. Ask for Clute. They know me. Everybody come!"

"Oh, we will!" "Trust us to be on hand for a meal!"

Luke went out on deck. The night was warm and dark, with clouds covering the moon. The village showed a few yellow lights; guitar music and singing drifted across the lagoon. Luke looked around for Carson, but failed to find him. He checked forward, among the deck passengers, without success. He went aft to the quarterdeck. No Carson. Luke frowned, pulled at his chin. He looked into the head, the saloon, then his own bunk, where Carson occasionally napped.

No sign of Carson.

Luke went forward once more, looked among the deck passengers. Titi was nowhere to be seen.

Aha, thought Luke. The situation was clarified.

He went to sit on the No. 2 hatch. But he became restless and uneasy. Exactly *where* was Carson? Luke rose indecisively to his feet. Carson would not take kindly to an intrusion; still, on the other hand…Luke walked aft, glanced into the port life-boat, to find only the pig and a terrible stench. He walked forward, around the other side of the deck-house, glanced into the starboard life-boat. Empty.

The captain's cabin? The crew's quarters? The hold? Aloft? Somewhat unlikely. Certainly not the roof of the forward deck-house. The roof of the after deck-house was more secluded.

Luke hesitated. Carson might be outraged. Luke went to the ladder, climbed three rungs, looked along the roof. "Oh! Sorry," said Luke, and jumped quickly back to the deck. He doubted if either had heard him.

Luke went forward. Leon Teofu sat with a friend. Both had guitars. The friend was teaching Leon chords to a tune Leon did not know. Leon sat absorbed, scowling in concentration as he placed his fingers, grinning in delight when the chords came right. He and his friend began to sing.

They finished the song. Leon looked around the deck. He craned his neck, looked more carefully. He put the guitar down, rose to his feet. Luke wondered what to do before the situation got out of hand. But now Titi came quietly along the deck, looking neither right nor left. She went to where her mother sat shelling and eating peanuts. She sat down in the shadows. Presently she ate a peanut.

Carson appeared from behind the after deck-house, a bland expression on his face. He looked toward Leon Teofu, then went back to the No. 2 hatch.

Leon Teofu sat muttering to his friend, who shrugged and began to play the guitar. Leon made a furious movement, raising and lowering his elbows, then, squatting, turned his back on Carson.

Luke exhaled with vast relief. He went to sit beside Carson. "I was looking for you."

"Oh? I was in the can. What's on your mind?"

"Clute is leaving the ship tomorrow. There'll be a vacant bunk."

Carson nodded with easy superiority. "It's already taken care of."

"I see. Well, that's all. Except…"

"Except what?"

"Nothing. Only…"

"Yes?"

"Forget it." Luke got to his feet, returned to the saloon. In his present mood, Carson would give only insufferable condescension to sound advice.

"I hope Teofu punches his head," said Luke to himself.

In the saloon Rolf Clute's brandy was having its effect. Clute was explaining how to capture a turtle. "They're old! They're pretty smart. They know things we don't know. If you bother them, they want to kill you. And what they try to do is catch you with their tail. Then they sink."

"Oh come now!" chortled Fiona. "Not really their tails!"

"That's the truth," declared Rolf Clute. "If they get you with their tail you're a dead man. You sit on the shell, you get a grip and hold their head up in the air and you can ride old grandpa for miles."

"Have you ever ridden a turtle?" Derek asked.

"Sure! In my younger days. I don't do it no more. I'm an old man now."

"Oh come, come," teased Fiona. "A person is as old as he feels. I saw you swimming after fish yesterday, with Mr. Easley."

"Oh well, that's different," said Clute modestly.

"I've always wanted to try my hand at it," remarked Derek. "Must be gorgeous, down among the coral. Pity you're leaving; I'd have you take me out."

"Nothing to it," said Clute. "Just don't put your hand in any holes. An eel might take off your fingers, or maybe your whole hand."

Fiona gave a muted cry of distress. "It's really disheartening! Everything lovely down here has a dreadful aspect just out of sight! As if the most beautiful flowers had poisonous scents!"

Clute shrugged. "That's the way it goes. This is a pretty savage part of the world. In the old days it was worse. Now if you just watch out for the stone-fish and the sting-rays and the poison shells and the *hue-hue*—"

"Don't forget the ghosts!" Derek inserted facetiously. "The *tupau-paus!*"

Fiona jumped to her feet. "I'll have nightmares if I listen another instant. So I'll take my constitutional twice around the deck, and then it's beddy-bye. Goodnight all!"

Rangiroa, the largest atoll of the Tuamotus, lay ahead. The outline of the reef was marked by narrow wooded islands; two villages were situated along the northern shore.

With diesel chugging the *Rahiria* pushed through a pass in the reef, crossed the lagoon to a weather-beaten concrete jetty. Behind lay Avatoru village: a mission school and a church, a small hospital built of coral-blocks, a Chinese grocery, a clapboard office-building, a number of thatched huts, all shaded under flamboyants, mangos, cocoanuts.

The *Rahiria* tied up to the pier. Rolf Clute, freshly shaven, glossy with talcum, in clean sun-tans and a new shirt, shook hands all around. "See everybody back at Tahiti! Don't forget!"

"Small chance of that," cried Fiona, and Derek called: "We'll be there, with bells on!"

Rolf Clute swaggered down the gangplank. About half of the deck passengers also disembarked, not including Titi and her relatives, nor Leon Teofu. Luke was disappointed.

Rolf Clute called up from the dock: "Don't swim in the lagoon: lots of sharks around here!" With a jaunty wave of the hand he went off into the village.

Stores were discharged, copra loaded. Avatoru, a straggling disorganized line of thatched huts, had small diversion to offer other than the grocery store and the ever-present church. The passengers stayed close to the ship. Early in the afternoon the *Rahiria* pulled aboard its lines, backed away from the pier and departed the way it had come.

Tikehau, the last port to be visited in the Tuamotus, lay eighteen miles west. A brisk breeze bellied the sails; the schooner plunged and rolled and left a fine bubbling wake. With the sun setting, the ship entered the pass into the lagoon and immediately anchored.

Without Rolf Clute the saloon was quiet and decorous, even though Carson had formally joined the group. Easley, never talkative, had become taciturn and preoccupied. What a fantastic position! thought Luke. A murderer customarily knew the identity of his unsuspecting victim. Here the situation was reversed: the murderer sat unaware that the victim watched him from across the table with a crawling skin.

During the evening Titi was carefully attended by her mother. Carson played gin rummy with the Orshams.

In the morning the *Rahiria* hoisted anchor and proceeded across the lagoon to Hirua village. There was no wharf at Hirua; the copra was brought out on a platform laid across two canoes.

The *Rahiria* would not depart until early afternoon, when the currents in the pass were favorable. The passengers went ashore in pirogues to explore the island. According to the natives there was no shark danger, and the Orshams went for a swim, as did the German students. Ben Easley borrowed the supercargo's spear-gun and mask and went off alone, ostensibly to fish.

Noon approached and passed; the passengers returned aboard: all but Easley. At one o'clock the *Rahiria* would sail, with Easley aboard or not. Luke borrowed the Orshams' binoculars, looked across the lagoon, but saw nothing. "Maybe he's been eaten by a shark," suggested Derek Orsham in a gentle voice.

Luke made a noncommittal sound and returned the binoculars.

At ten minutes to one Easley came sauntering along the beach. Without haste he engaged a native boy to paddle him to the ship and climbed the ladder just as the captain ordered up the anchor.

The ship put to sea, and headed northeast, with the wind on the starboard beam. The Tuamotus were astern. Ahead, across six hundred miles of empty ocean, lay the Marquesas.

CHAPTER XV

THE TIME WAS AN HOUR before dawn. Brady stood on deck with his sextant watching the sky take on color. The constellations had not yet faded from sight; Brady picked his stars and waited for the horizon to take an edge.

The wind was cool and gentle; the *Dorado* moved quietly over the dark water. This was the time of day when Brady felt most at peace. Guests, relatives, friends: all very well, no doubt, but their idiosyncrasies tended to grate on the nerves. If through some trick of fate he ever found himself single again, he might just chuck it all for a life of solitary voyaging. Unlikely that events would proceed so far, nor would he want them to do so...Brady found himself thinking about Jean Wintersea. Several times during the last few days he had surprised her watching him with fascinated attention: a circumstance which puzzled Brady. His sex appeal? Hmmf, said Brady to himself. High time that he was taking his sights. He stepped into the chart-room, started his stopwatch by the chronometer, went back out on deck and took an angle on Achernar.

Half an hour later he transferred his fix to the general chart, considered it a moment, then swept the forward horizon with his binoculars. Nothing in sight. He descended to the saloon where Hector served him coffee and orange juice. He was presently joined by Malcolm McClure. "Nine o'clock," said Brady. "To be absolutely precise, let's say eight forty-five."

"I'll be watching."

At ten minutes to nine the dimmest of shadows appeared on the southern horizon. Malcolm McClure was the first to see it, and gave a great halloo. "Nuku Hiva! Right on the nose! Everybody up! Marquesas landfall!"

"That's what I call precise navigating," said Brady.

"Pretty lucky," said McClure.

One by one the passengers came to peer and marvel, as if never had they seen land before.

The shadow rose into the sky and presently became a succession of great promontories, each the size of a mountain, receding one behind the other into the haze of distance. At noon the *Dorado* rounded Cape Martin and proceeded along the south coast with McClure comparing the chart with the landscape. "See that ledge? With the surf bashing over the top? That's called Teohote Kea… Look through there! That's Comptroller Bay. There ahead: Sentinel Rocks. We go between into Taio Hae Bay, our port of entry."

Flying the quarantine flag, the *Dorado* slid past Sentinel Rocks into the shelter of the bay. To all sides rose the incredible peaks and spires of Nuku Hiva.

Down rattled the sails. The *Dorado* lost way. The anchor splashed into clear cool water. The schooner, for the first time since leaving Honolulu, was at rest.

Ten minutes later a launch brought out port officials. They made a perfunctory examination of passports, the ship's log, and without further formality granted pratique.

Cocoanut toddy had been brought aboard the *Rahiria* at Tikehau. On the first evening out the deck passengers became extremely merry. The guitars generated an urgent emotion; there was laughter, hand-clapping, singing, the *tamure*.

The saloon passengers came forward to enjoy the fun, bringing what tipple they had available: the Orshams a bottle of Scotch; the Germans a jug of red wine; Luke, Carson and Easley, Hinano beer purchased from the supercargo.

Carson edged close to Titi, who pretended to ignore him. Leon Teofu, red-eyed from an excess of toddy, was not inclined to do so and began to stagger to his feet. Luke recognized the incipient stages of Polynesian rage. He quickly took Carson's arm and pulled him away.

"What's the matter with you?" demanded Carson peevishly. "I wasn't doing anything out of line."

"Leon thought you were."

Carson made a sour noise. "Bah. I can take care of myself. Do you think I'm a damn fool?"

"You know I do. Take my advice and leave that girl alone."

"I can't see what harm I'm doing. She doesn't object, her mother doesn't object — not too much. I don't object."

"But Leon objects. Do you intend to marry the girl?"

"Heaven forbid."

"Maybe Leon does. For heaven's sake, control yourself. You can't go waylaying every girl you see."

"It's worked out pretty well so far," growled Carson. "Now if you don't mind…"

Luke held up his hands. "I'm finished. You're on your own. If you get your teeth knocked out, don't come to me for sympathy."

"Don't worry," muttered Carson, and strode off in a huff.

But for the remainder of the evening he sulked by himself on the edge of the hatch, as discreet as even Luke could have wished: to such an extent that Titi began to turn teasing glances toward him.

The toddy ran short; the revellers began to fall asleep: the music dwindled to plaintive chords and single plangent notes. The Orshams bade everyone goodnight and took their Scotch back to their cabin, followed by the Germans and Ben Easley.

Luke rose to his feet. He looked expectantly toward Carson, who reluctantly came aft.

During the night Ching had a nightmare and called out hysterically in Chinese.

Luke leaned over his bunk. "Ching! Wake up! Ching! Hey!"

Ching's outburst ended in a gasp of sheer terror, then he lay back on the pillow breathing heavily.

"Ching! Are you all right?"

Ching made a sleepy inarticulate sound; somewhat reassured Luke lay back down in his bunk and adjusted himself once more to the slow heave of the ship.

✳

At breakfast Carson had little to say, and brooded sullenly over his bread and coffee. Luke divined that Carson resented the restrictions Luke and Leon Teofu had imposed upon his love life.

Luke left him to stew in his own juice and went out on deck with a book he had borrowed from the Orshams.

Ten minutes later Carson appeared on deck. He stood a moment by the rail, glowering at the hillocks of blue water, then he turned and swaggered forward.

Titi lay on the forward hatch, face down, basking. Her hair was tumbled artlessly to one side of her neck; she wore a faded old cotton dress, covering her brown legs to the backs of her knees.

Carson sat down beside her, arms clasping his own knees. He looked somberly out to sea. Now that he was here, now that he had defied Luke and Leon Teofu, he could think of nothing further he cared to accomplish at the moment.

Titi watched through her lashes, thinking her own thoughts, none very profound. She rather liked Carson. Leon was also good enough in his way.

Carson began a conversation in halting French. Leon Teofu, playing cards with three cronies, kept an attentive eye on the situation. One of his comrades made a joke. Leon scowled, then uttered a short bark of a laugh. Then he relaxed and laughed more easily. Then he scowled once more. Leon Teofu was examining all sides of the situation.

For the moment he decided to continue with the card game.

Easley came out on deck, looked briefly this way and that, went aft to the quarterdeck, sprawled in a deck-chair.

Titi raised up on her elbows, and kicking her legs up in the air, began to take an interest in the conversation. She laughed at Carson's drollery.

Carson glanced aft, speculated a moment, licked his lips. He turned, muttered to Titi, who gave her head a vigorous shake.

Carson spoke again; Titi's response was not so emphatic, and was followed by a glance toward her mother.

Carson spoke once more, then jumped to his feet, sauntered casually aft and into his cabin.

He waited. A moment passed. Were those angry words out on deck?

He listened, but heard nothing more. Probably only the timbers of the old ship.

Quiet footsteps sounded outside. There was a tap at the door. Carson threw it open.

A terrible mistake! Leon Teofu, not Titi, stood looking at him.

Leon punched Carson's face, to send him hopping back into the cabin. Then Leon called Carson names in Tahitian, and shook his fist.

Carson sprang forward in rage, but Leon Teofu had already turned away. Carson wiped his mouth with the back of his hand and went off in pursuit. Leon turned. Carson was on him with a wild flurry of blows. Leon grinned, pushed his left fist into Carson's face. Carson tottered back, then once again rushed forward. He managed to hit Leon once or twice; then, in backing away, Leon tripped on a pad-eye and fell. Carson stood over him like a lord. "And there's plenty more where that came from!" shouted Carson furiously.

Leon Teofu picked himself up, but before he could make any new move the captain appeared, and peremptorily ordered Leon back. Then he turned a stinging spatter of French upon Carson and shook his finger under Carson's nose.

Carson went to sit on the hatch. Leon Teofu conducted an angry conversation with his friends, glaring from time to time toward Carson, who glowered back.

Luke, lounging in a deck-chair with his book, pretended not to notice the episode.

The afternoon passed. Dinner was as usual: canned beef with rice and fried sweet potatoes, together with grilled dorado, caught on a trolling line by the supercargo.

Tonight guitar music was absent from the foredeck. Clouds hung over the *Rahiria* and the deck passengers were worried about rain, which so far had been limited to one or two brief swishes. The sky seemed heavy and the air humid. In the west lightning crackled.

But the rain held off. One by one the deck passengers crawled into their bedrolls.

The Orshams and Luke sat in the saloon until almost midnight, sipping the Orshams' Scotch by the light of the kerosene lamp.

All finally turned in. There was little wind, and this came in panting damp little gusts, which barely gave the schooner headway.

Luke was awakened by a sound. He listened. What had he heard? He could not recall.

He raised up on his elbow, strained his ears, his heart beating as if he were a little boy awakening from a nightmare.

Silence, except for the surge of water and the sigh of wind. From the bunk below came the sound of Ching's breathing.

A door closed.

Luke lay staring into the dark, wondering why he felt awed and terrified.

The ship surged on, heaving up, easing down over unseen hills and vales of water. Luke fell into a troubled slumber.

First to breakfast was Ching, then the Orshams, then Luke and the Germans.

Ben Easley came late to the saloon. Fiona remarked saucily that he and Carson were slug-a-beds and deserved to miss their breakfasts.

Easley laughed. He seemed in an excellent good mood. "Me, yes. Carson, no. He's been up for hours."

"Ha ha! He must be out on deck, mooning over that little trol-lop—if one may so refer to undisciplined Polynesians."

But Carson was not on deck. In fact Carson was nowhere aboard the *Rahiria*.

Carson was gone.

"When a man disappears from a ship," said Derek, "there's only one place for him to go."

The captain, uttering staccato French oaths through a down-clenched mouth, ordered the *Rahiria* back on its course. He put one man at the masthead, another at the bow, while he himself stood on the forward deck-house with binoculars. The search obviously was a forlorn hope; among the great surges, reaching from horizon to horizon, how could such a small entity, even one so warm and desperate as a swimming man, be seen?

But the search was made.

All morning long the *Rahiria* roved back the way it had come, with everybody aboard standing by the rail, scanning every slope of water, every sudden view along a trough.

At noon the captain flung up his hands in a Gallic gesture, and ordered the ship back on course. Everyone looked at him reproachfully, though everyone knew that he had no remedy for the situation.

Titi lay weeping on the hatch while her mother clucked beside her. Leon Teofu sat gray-faced to the side, aware that all the ship's company were giving him glances of surreptitious speculation.

All except Luke. He watched Ben Easley, who lounged on the quarterdeck in a deck-chair. Easley wore dark glasses, white shorts, a white shirt. He held a long thin cigar. From time to time he puffed, then emitted a small stream of smoke through his pursed lips to be whisked away by the wind.

Luke could not bear to look at him, for the acrid lump of fury which rose in his throat. He had never thought it possible to hate a man as much as he hated Ben Easley.

First Luke Royce, then Carson Royce. And Ben Easley was on his way to meet the *Dorado*, on which rode Brady Royce.

The situation was significant, thought Luke. First Luke and Carson, then Brady, whereupon there would be no further Royces to administer the Golconda Fund.

Lia Wintersea Royce would be named administratrix.

From Ben Easley's point of view, the situation was proceeding with facility. Two-thirds of his work was done. Carson's appearance at Papeete, his presence aboard the *Rahiria*, his difficulties with Leon Teofu: these must have seemed the dispensation of an amiable if bloodthirsty god.

There was a single fatal flaw in the scheme. Eventually Ben Easley must face up to a staggering fact: he had not, after all, killed Luke Royce.

And once Luke had a chance to speak two words to Brady, the whole scheme would evaporate in a flash.

Luke thought of something else. If Brady were dead, he, Luke, would become administrator: lord of Golconda, master of the *Dorado*, with unlimited wealth at his disposal ... Luke smiled: a small harsh smile. He felt soiled by the thought, yet why should he blame himself? The idea was one which loomed into the mind.

Leon Teofu was under suspicion. The captain and the supercargo spoke together at length; then the captain called first Titi, then Ben Easley, into his cabin and questioned each in turn: had Titi seen Carson during the night? Had she observed anyone from among the deck passengers, specifically Leon Teofu, heading aft?

Titi had slept soundly. She had seen nothing, heard nothing.

Ben Easley said the same. He had gone to his bunk, he had slept. In the morning the top bunk was empty. He knew no more.

No sounds, no outcries, no scuffle?

Easley could not help.

One by one the other passengers were questioned. All declared that they had heard and seen nothing.

Leon Teofu burst into a furious tirade. He knew that everyone suspected him of a foul deed. He was innocent! He was not a man of the night; he went to his enemies by day and confronted them face to face! Whoever declared otherwise: let the slanderer beware!

The captain shrugged. *"Eh bien.* We will turn the matter over to the authorities. They will know how to deal with the matter." He would proceed directly to Taio Hae Bay on Nuku Hiva, instead of putting into Hiva Oa, as had been his schedule.

Chapter XVI

The wind died to a whisper. Overhead hung a huge bank of black and grey clouds, ordinarily the signal for a thrashing rain-squall. But the air barely moved, as if the sky were holding its breath. What with the circumstances aboard the *Rahiria*, the effect was one of awful portentousness.

Luke wondered if Easley felt the oppression. If so, Easley gave no sign. He sat aft in the deck-chair, smoking his thin cigar. When he looked astern, what did he see?

There was a belated lunch. The Orshams picked despondently at their food. Luke ate a banana and drank two cups of tea. Easley lunched as usual, with a thoughtful pause from time to time. Luke could not bring himself to look into Easley's face. Easley, as a rule indifferent, seemed to sense Luke's emotion, and from time to time turned him a curious glance.

Luke thought: he wonders if I know something no one else knows. He wonders what I have seen or heard. He is casting back, reviewing the events, trying to calculate just how much I know, if anything.

Easley heaved a small sigh, once more addressed himself to his plate.

On Saturday morning the black peaks of Nuku Hiva appeared over the horizon. At midmorning the *Rahiria* sailed into Taio Hae Bay.

Borrowing the Orshams' binoculars Luke scanned the reach of dark water. In various quarters four yachts were at anchor. None was the *Dorado*.

Luke put down the binoculars. The *Dorado* had certainly arrived at the Marquesas. Brady would naturally prefer not to anchor at Taio Hae, the most frequented port of the islands. He would seek out an isolated cove, under great black crags, near one of the famous Marquesan cataracts.

A letter or a message of some kind presumably awaited Luke, with instructions as to how to join the ship.

The water of the bay was like a dark green mirror. The *Rahiria* eased with hardly a ripple up to the pier at the head of the bay. The sails came down; mooring lines were made fast to the dock.

"Everyone must remain aboard the ship," said the captain. "I will consult with the authorities."

The port commissioner and the commandant of the gendarmerie returned aboard the *Rahiria* with the captain: the commissioner a plump Frenchman with a gray toothbrush mustache, the commandant a massive white-haired Marquesan with a face carved from teak. They closeted themselves with the captain for twenty minutes, then called in the passengers, one by one. Ching Piao was first. He was dismissed almost immediately and went ashore. Next the Germans were called; they too were allowed to disembark. Easley was next. Luke paced back and forth, wondering what Easley would say, but more immediately concerned by the dilemma in which he found himself. Was he 'Jim Harrison' or was he 'Luke Royce'? In either case he faced a potential embarrassment.

Luke paced and pondered. 'Easley' — actually Benjamin Eiselhardt — was in something of the same fix. But Easley sauntered from the cabin, showing no sign of embarrassment. Luke turned sharply away. Easley went ashore.

The Orshams were questioned next: first Fiona, then Derek. Finally Luke was summoned into the cabin. The commissioner looked hot and rumpled and disgusted with the whole proceeding. The commandant sat to the side, stolid as a stump. He fixed his eyes upon Luke's face and never moved them, with unnerving effect.

Luke's dilemma was resolved at once. "Passport, please."

Luke heaved a sigh, pushed it across the table.

"Hmm. Luke Royce." The commissioner raised his eyebrows. "You are related to the lost man?"

"We are cousins."

"Indeed. Well, then, what can you tell me regarding the tragic circumstances?"

"Nothing. I went to bed; when I awoke Carson was gone."

"I see." The commissioner glanced at a sheet of paper. "Who then is 'Jim Harrison'?"

This was the question Luke had been hoping to avoid. "In Papeete there was a person I wanted to avoid — someone from the States. I called myself 'Jim Harrison' because I was afraid she might follow me aboard the *Rahiria*."

The commissioner gave a soft snort of derision, but did not pursue the subject. "How do you account for your cousin's disappearance?"

"I have no idea. As you probably know, he had a quarrel with one of the deck passengers, but I can't believe that the man would push Carson overboard on that account. It's totally unreasonable."

The commissioner gave a noncommittal jerk of the head. "What of suicide? Was your cousin in poor spirits?"

"No, I wouldn't say so. I can't imagine him killing himself."

The commissioner grunted, and spoke in French to the commandant, who returned a few gruff words.

The commissioner turned back to Luke. "Can you tell us anything more?"

"I wish I could." For a moment Luke was tempted to blurt out everything: all his suspicions, all his inferences. He restrained himself. He could prove nothing; to act hastily would startle his quarry. His first and urgent task was to locate Brady Royce. "Has the schooner *Dorado* arrived from Honolulu?"

"Several days ago, perhaps a week."

"Where is it anchored now?"

The commissioner gave a shrug and rustled his papers. "I do not know."

"Did the captain leave a letter in your care for me?"

"No." He pursed his lips, pulled at his mustache. "The subject was mentioned. I suggested that the post office offered a convenient service."

"I see. Where is the post office?"

"Next to the Englishman's store. But it will be closed by now, or so I suspect, since it is Saturday afternoon. Perhaps if you hurry, you will find the postmaster on the premises."

Luke left the cabin in haste. He ran down the gangplank, to stand looking this way and that. Two heavy-faced women in limp white dresses and palm-frond hats turned to stare at Luke, then continued on their way chuckling. Luke realized that he must cut a ridiculous figure. But no matter! Where was the post office?

A hundred yards north, tall trees shaded a row of frame buildings with rusty corrugated metal roofs. Luke set off up the road at a half-trot. Easley stood at the end of the dock inspecting a trimaran moored by fore and aft lines: a ketch-rigged craft perhaps thirty-five feet long, with an intriguing little stern-cabin. An Australian flag drooped from the stays.

As Luke passed, Easley looked around, then with insulting deliberacy turned back to his contemplation of the boat.

Luke gritted his teeth. Easley recognized his detestation, but clearly couldn't care less.

Luke stopped in front of a store with a faded sign reading: McDermot, Merchandiser. A half-dozen Marquesans of various ages sat on benches outside or squatted, smoking and talking. Taking note of Luke, they became quiet, turning their heads to watch him. A different people from the amiable Tahitians, thought Luke: these were a brooding, heavy-minded folk, oppressed by their tragic history.

Next to the store was a small frame building: the post office.

Luke tried the door. It was locked. He gave the door-knob a rattle, stood back in disgust. The Marquesans watched with faint smiles for Luke's discomfiture. A young man with peculiarly red hair curled tightly against his head murmured, *"Fermée."*

Luke gave a curt nod, and went to sit on a bench at the end of the porch. What to do next? Around Nuku Hiva's shoreline were a dozen delightful coves and bays where the *Dorado* might be anchored. A pair of other islands were little more than an hour's sail away: Ua Huka to the east, Ua Pu to the south. Brady might have taken the *Dorado* across to Hiva Oa, the largest and most beautiful island of the group. In the absence of information there were no decisions to be made. It might be instructive, thought Luke, to watch Ben Easley and learn something of his plans.

But first, a try at the Marquesans. He crossed the porch: as before they halted their conversation, to look at him with faintly hostile indifference.

Luke spoke in his halting French: *"Connaissez-vous la grande goélette Dorado?"*

The young man with the red hair said, *"Oui, monsieur. La goélette Dorado, je connais."*

"Où est-elle, savez-vous?"

"Elle est partie. Maintenant — je ne sais pas. Peut-être Hiva Oa. Peut-être Tahiti."

"Merci, monsieur." Luke walked back down the road toward the dock, more slowly than he had come. The trimaran had set sail, he noted, and was skimming easily over the smooth bay. Easley no longer stood on the dock.

Apprehension stabbed Luke. He ran back down the road, stopping short as the Orshams came past. "Where is Easley?"

Derek Orsham facetiously raised his eyebrows at Luke's brusqueness. He pointed to the trimaran. Luke's worst fears were confirmed. "He picked up a letter at the post office — something about a boat he expected to meet. Then he dickered for a ride with the trimaran fellows and off they went."

Luke stared after the dwindling sails. He asked: "How did he get a letter? The post office is closed."

"I fancy it was open when he went ashore. Must have closed shortly after."

Luke turned and raced back to the store. He approached the red-haired man. *"Où est la maison du maître de poste, connaissez-vous?"*

"Oui, monsieur." The man made an indifferent gesture up the valley. *"Là-haut."*

"Montrez-moi, s'il vous plaît. Je vous paie cinq cents francs."

"Cinq cents francs?" The Marquesan considered. He looked sidelong at his fellows. They gave him no signal. He temporized: *"Voulez-vous y aller maintenant?"*

"Oui, monsieur, tout de suite. C'est très important."

The young man rose languidly to his feet, shook his head to his companions in wry derogation. *"Bon, allons-y."*

He led the way up the road toward the head of the bay. In and out of the dank shade they walked, through the glaring contrasts of sunlight and gloom which distinguished the Marquesas Islands from Tahiti, where the air was open, the light even. The red-haired man turned aside into a lane angling up toward a cleft in the black crags. They walked in a melancholy hush punctuated by bird calls; foliage pressed in on them: tree ferns, breadfruit, *mape*, an occasional banana palm, ti plants with broad heart-shaped leaves. At irregular intervals paths led to thatched huts, each on its ancient stone *paepae*.

The red-headed man turned up one of those paths, jumped aside as a raw-boned cur leapt out to the end of its chain. With fangs gnashing the air only inches from their legs, Luke and his guide sidled past the dog and approached a thatch hut differing from the others only in the motor-scooter parked on the *paepae*. A girl of fourteen or fifteen came to the door, gnawing at a chunk of cold breadfruit. The red-haired man spoke in the Marquesan dialect; she glanced sullenly at Luke, shrugged, uttered a few words, then took another bite of breadfruit as the red-haired man turned to Luke. *"Pas ici."*

"Où est-il? C'est très important que je le voie."

The red-haired man spoke again to the girl. She nodded toward Luke and spoke at somewhat greater length.

The red-haired man turned to Luke once again. *"Vous n'êtes pas français, n'est-ce pas?"*

"Non, non! Je suis américain."

A new colloquy with the girl: this time she gave grudging directions. The two men returned to the lane.

The red-haired man spoke over his shoulder: *"Le maître de poste, il visite ses amis."* He made a motion as of drinking, and looked furtively up the lane. *"Les Français —"* he made a gesture indicating contemptuous disapproval, and Luke nodded in comprehension. Cocoanut toddy, the illicit brew derived from the flowing sap of the cocoanut palm, was far more potent than it tasted, and likewise went untaxed, as did orange beer.

The red-haired man led the way along a dark path which ran beside a patch of vanilla vines, crossed a meadow where a half-dozen brown Marquesan ponies grazed, then up the mountainside. Muffled through the foliage Luke heard the throb of a rather out-of-tune guitar, then a murmur of voices. Presently they came to a large *paepae* with a ramshackle hut at the back from which came smoke, the reek of frying fish and garlic. On the ancient stones sat two dozen men and women drinking toddy and orange beer: the first milky pale, the second the color of diluted orange juice. To the side lounged a dozen young bucks with pomaded hair, who laughed and joked but did no drinking. Luke wondered at their restraint.

At the sight of Luke the group immediately became rigid. Scowls appeared; someone uttered a gruff challenge. The red-haired man called out; there was an exchange of conversation; Luke heard the word *Rahiria*. Then a portly man in gray trousers and a gray shirt rose to his feet, came unsteadily down from the *paepae*.

To Luke's gratification he spoke English with a furry, half-French, half-Marquesan accent. "Yes sir. I am the master of the post. You want to find me, eh?"

"Yes. My name is Luke Royce. I think you have a letter for me at the post office."

"A letter is there. For Mr. Luke Royce. The post office is closed. I close it myself. On Monday I open it myself."

"The letter is very important," said Luke. "I'll pay you, say, a thousand francs to open up and give me the letter."

"No. That is against the rule. The French are very — how you say, *pointilleux*."

The red-haired man had quietly accepted a glass of toddy, and now he took another which he handed to Luke. The postmaster climbed with sodden dignity back up to the *paepae*, where he sat pointedly ignoring Luke.

"*Attendez un petit peu,*" whispered the red-haired man. "*Il boit beaucoup. Après — peut-être qu'il vous donnera votre lettre. Buvez avec lui. Il pensera que vous êtes son cher ami.*"

The advice, that Luke should drink with the postmaster until that official in an excess of camaraderie should totter to the post office and give Luke his letter, seemed far-fetched. But Luke had no better plan in mind. He climbed up on the *paepae* and seated himself on a bench. The toddy tasted like acrid cocoanut milk, not at all unpleasant. Luke sipped it cautiously. Not so the Marquesans, who drank enormous competitive gulps, as if each hoped to become more thoroughly drunk than his fellow. In the cook-house older women were working, without pleasure; from time to time a spate of angry words could be heard. Presently two girls carried forth platters heaped with what appeared to be fish balls and offered them among the celebrants. Luke took the smallest on the platter and found it to be more garlic than fish. The postmaster ate hugely and drank orange beer to match. As yet he showed no tendency to regard Luke as an old drinking buddy, and Luke began to wonder if, when totally drunk, his opinion would change.

Luke became restless. He drank the toddy, looked at his watch, studied the postmaster, who now had removed his gray shirt to reveal a perspiration-stained undershirt and huge brown arms.

Luke's impatience became overpowering. The *Dorado* might already have departed for Hiva Oa, the *Rahiria's* next port of call. But no; in this case Ben Easley would hardly have sailed off in the trimaran. The *Dorado* must be relatively close at hand.

Luke could no longer contain himself. He jumped to his feet, approached the postmaster, and ingenuously put his request, as if it were a sudden new idea.

The postmaster blinked glassy eyes, barely comprehending. Luke added an inducement: "I'll buy you a bottle of whiskey!"

"Letter comes Monday. You bring bottle of whiskey Monday."

Luke made a gesture of despair, jumped down from the *paepae*. The red-haired man showed no disposition to leave. Luke paid over five hundred francs and set off alone down the dank path. Only the young men with the oiled hair took note of his departure. Then once more they watched the drinkers, waiting until one or another of the women would stumble into the undergrowth to relieve herself.

Seething with frustration Luke returned down the lane to Taio Hae village. He looked along the wharf: the trimaran had not returned. Luke cursed under his breath. He halted in front of the post office, peered through the dusty windows, hoping against hope to find an assistant or underling working overtime. The office was empty save for a dozen large wasps. Luke returned to the *Rahiria*. The cargo had been discharged; sacks of copra were being loaded aboard.

The Orshams had been taking photographs of the copra-loading. "Have a nice jaunt?" Fiona asked brightly. "Boat's about ready to leave," said Derek. "We feared that you'd be left ashore."

"Mr. Easley went for a sail," said Fiona, "and he's nowhere in view. I'm sure he'll miss departure."

"I'm staying here as well," said Luke.

"What?" cried Fiona. "Our little group is breaking up so soon?"

"I'm meeting some friends on a yacht," Luke explained. "I'd better get off my luggage. What have the police been doing?"

"Interviewing deck passengers and the crew," said Derek. "No one admits to a thing, though everyone blames that surly Leon Teofu."

"Yes, he's a bit of a beast, isn't he?" Fiona remarked.

"Still — he claims innocence," Derek pointed out. "The girl gives him an alibi."

"Declares that they were sleeping together, sly little basket!"

"Hmmf," said Luke. "Under the circumstances there's not much to be done. It's hard to investigate when there's no evidence, no witnesses, nothing."

"Not even a corpse," murmured Derek.

"Poor Carson!" cried Fiona. "A shame, a dreadful shame!"

CHAPTER XVII

THE *RAHIRIA* HAD SAILED from Taio Hae Bay. Already the events aboard were diminishing. The faces seemed vague, the sounds remote, Carson's disappearance an unlikely nightmare.

At the rooming house annexed to the Englishman's store, Luke was taken to a room at the back overlooking the chicken-yard. He put his suitcase on the bed and went to the front porch. There was a sail on the bay. Luke recognized the trimaran *Banshee*.

He ran down the road to the wharf, and stood waiting. The wind was slight; the trimaran eased toward the dock with maddening deliberation. Two figures sat in the cockpit. Neither was Ben Easley.

Fifty yards offshore the man at the tiller flung out the anchor, paying off line as the trimaran slid up to the wharf. The second man stood on the foredeck with a coil of line. He called to Luke: "Hey, matey, lend a hand, there's a good chap." He tossed over the line. "Just make fast to the bollard."

Luke hitched the line as directed. He spoke to the man on the foredeck, now lowering the mainsail. "Did you just take a man to the *Dorado*?"

"Couldn't be righter," said the seaman. "Friend of yours?"

"In a way. Where did you take him?"

"Round the coast, place called Tai Oa Bay. Regular little Garden of Eden."

"Even got some nymphs," said the Australian aft. "Saw a couple aboard the *Dorado*. Queer feeling; I'd almost forgotten what a white girl looks like."

"Will you take me to the *Dorado*?" asked Luke. "I'll pay the going rate."

"It's the Banshee Bloody Ferry Service we are," groused the man forward. "But if you pays the money, you gets the ride. Right, Bob?"

"Right. Morning will suit, no doubt?"

"I want to go now."

"Can't be done, bucko. There's no wind out yonder."

"Don't you have an engine?" demanded Luke. "I've got to get to the *Dorado* as soon as possible."

"We've got a ruddy fine engine," said Bob. "One thing wrong: no fuel."

"Two things wrong. The bugger won't start."

Luke looked out across the bay. He pointed to a cat's-paw. "Surely there's wind enough! It can't be more than a few miles."

"Seven miles by the chart. But notice, old chum, it's close to sundown. Hard on Tai Oa inlet is a rock, long as Sydney Bridge, ugly as the opera house. What chance do we have in the dark? Hey, Mike?"

"With that current? A farthing's worth."

"In the morning, matey. Right now it's time for a bottle of beer, providing the Englishman got in his cargo."

Luke returned to the rooming house. Two girls were tending the store: the Englishman's gold-toothed daughter and a Chinese girl. Luke leaned on the counter. "How can I get to Tai Oa Bay? Is there a road?"

The girls giggled as if Luke had propounded the riddle of the Sphinx. "No road, sir," said the daughter in quaintly accented English. "Only the path up the valley, then back down into Tai Oa Valley. You'd never get a horse this time of day. If you walked you'd be sure to lose yourself; it's all of ten miles just up and down the crags."

"Give me a bottle of beer," said Luke through gritted teeth. He noticed the Australians trudging up the road toward the store. "Make it three bottles."

The Australians entered the store, to stand back in gratified shock when Luke handed each a bottle of Hinano beer. "This makes the day!" declared Mike, a round-faced young man with a fringe of ginger-colored hair encircling his face.

"An absolute stroke of luck! Don't happen often enough!" stated Bob, who was tough and stocky, with a corded ugly face, a stubble of yellow hair.

"Cheers!" "Cheers!"

"Cheers," said Luke. "Let's sit down on the bench. Something I want to ask you."

"Ask away, we've got nothing to hide!"

"You took Easley directly to the *Dorado*?"

"Correct!"

"He went aboard?"

"Correct!"

"Did he speak to anyone? Did anyone call him by name?"

"Didn't hardly notice, I was so busy with the bevy of beauties. Seems to me it was the captain who piped the man aboard. What do you say, Mike?"

"Well, it was something different. Easley — that's the bloke's name? — he was standing by the mast, looking toward the boat. One of the women saw him — it was almost like she was watching for him. She went to talk to the captain. He came to the accommodation ladder and Easley went aboard."

"I see. Which woman was it?"

"I don't know any of 'em by name, matey. Wish I did. All was really smashers."

"Well, what did she look like?"

"Bang-up. A bit of all right, as the saying goes. How do you call 'em in the States? A real pip."

"Thought old Mike's eyes would bulge clear out," said Bob.

"Did you hear anybody speak to Easley?"

"No, can't say as I did."

"There was some talk," said Bob, "but it didn't register. The usual type chatter, man coming aboard ship and all. 'How de do' and 'Welcome aboard' and 'What a surprise to see you' and that sort of thing."

"Who said it was a surprise?"

"One of the ladies; but it wasn't the one that ran to the captain."

"Anything else that you noticed?"

"No. We sheered right off and came back to Taio Hae. We still lack clearance from Papeete; probably won't get the word until Monday morning."

"Yeah, the Frenchies give everybody a clean bill of health before they let 'em in. Don't want no agitators or unsavory types."

"Our goose is cooked right there," said Mike. "What did you say your name was?"

"I'm Luke Royce."

"Pleased to meet you. I'm Mike Hannigan; there's Bob Higgins… Come to think of it, the captain on the *Dorado* mentioned a Luke. He says to Easley: 'You're just in from Papeete?' And Easley says, 'Right ho.' And the captain says, 'Was Luke on the boat?' And Easley says, 'Never heard of no Luke!' Words to that effect."

Luke groaned in dismay.

"Speaking of women," said Bob, "did you notice the dollies in the store? Maybe we'll have a party after all."

"A bit young, my boy. Still showing their milk teeth."

"You're right, of course. Well, you sit out here and yarn with Luke. I want to do a bit of shopping."

"Not so fast. Which one do you favor?"

"I rather fancy her in the pink dress with the gold tooth."

"In the best of taste. A real smasher. I'll settle for the other. A jolly little soul, no doubt. Just my type."

"Where does that leave poor Luke?"

"Luke can carry the picnic basket. Let's go give it a whirl."

The two went into the store. Mike said, "Think we'll make a large purchase: three more bottles of beer, and what would you ladies like to drink?"

"Nothing, sir, nothing at all."

"Oh come now. Surely you wouldn't want to hurt our feelings? Do you like beer?"

"Oh no!"

"Never touch the stuff, eh? Well, you're right. Bob here has swilled the stuff all his days. Look what a wreck it's made of him."

"He doesn't look so bad!"

"No matter how he looks, he's still kind to his mother. Incidentally, this is Saturday night. What goes on in the way of social activity?"

"Nothing. Just a dance at the Mormon mission."

"Wonderful! Maybe you girls would take us over. Always wanted to meet a Mormon."

"Susy can't go," said the Englishman's daughter. "Chinese people are very strict."

"Worse than the Mormons?"

"I don't know about that."

"Does Susy speak English?"

"No. Just French."

"Ask her if she can leave the house by the back door."

"Oh no! Her father would beat her."

"Well, Bob," said Mike, "I fear you'll have to watch the store with Susy…Unless — what's your name?"

"I'm Angel."

"Unless Angel has another beautiful friend. What about it, Angel?"

"There'll be girls at the mission."

With nothing better to do, Luke also went to the dance, and stood for an hour or so watching the couples dancing prim foxtrots to records. The affair was strictly chaperoned. On the grounds of the mission sat several dozen young men in glistening white shirts, drinking wine and calling out to the girls, to the intense disapproval of the missionaries. Mike and Bob behaved far better than Luke had expected, dancing with propriety and arousing little suspicion from the missionaries.

Luke left early and he had no knowledge of how the evening ended.

Returning to the rooming house he looked out on a weirdly beautiful sight. The night was dark; the crags loomed black against the stars. Out on the bay drifted dozens of pirogues, each with a flickering torch held over the water. Luke went to his room, undressed, stretched out on the bed. Last night he had slept aboard the *Rahiria*: a time already an aeon distant.

He awoke early, to crowing and cackling from the chicken-yard. Mist clung to the lower slopes of the crags; a cool mother-of-pearl light seemed to rise from the bay.

The surface of the water was dead calm. Luke went back to bed, and dozed another hour or two.

The Englishman's wife served a hearty breakfast: canned bacon, eggs, fried bananas, a huge hemisphere of Polynesian grapefruit, Marquesan coffee. Luke ate without appetite, and was presently joined by Mike and Bob who seemed a trifle subdued.

Luke inquired when they could leave for Tai Oa.

"Anytime," replied Mike. "There's not much breeze but once we reach the ocean we'll catch a wind."

The wind was ample for the feather-light trimaran. It skimmed out of the bay on a single tack, veered between the Sentinels and turned west with the wind dead astern.

The crags and peaks of Nuku Hiva shifted past. Mike pointed ahead to a set of vertical pinnacles. "That's the entrance to Tai Oa Bay. Here." He passed Luke the binoculars. "Look below."

Luke saw a long half-submerged ledge half across the opening upon which the ocean swells seethed and swirled. Mike and Bob were vindicated. A sail through the dark into Tai Oa Bay with little or no wind would have been foolhardy.

The *Banshee* sailed past the entrance, jibed, slid deftly through the entrance. Luke went to stand on the foredeck. The bay was split into a pair of coves. Heavy dark green foliage came down to white sand beaches; from crags to right and left hung the famous Marquesan cataracts. Two yachts lay at anchor. Neither was the *Dorado*.

"That's odd," said Mike. "She seems to have disappeared."

"Not disappeared, old man: simply sailed away."

Luke spoke in a carefully controlled voice. "Naturally you're sure that this is the right place?"

"Heavens yes. She was hooked over yonder, near that blue yawl."

Luke gave a deep sigh. No mystery what had happened. Brady, informed that Luke had not been aboard the *Rahiria*, had hoisted anchor and set sail for Tahiti.

They approached the spot where the *Dorado* had lain at anchor, in thirty feet of water as clear as air, with white sand and occasional growths of orange and blue and purple coral below. The yawl was the *Viviane* out of Santa Monica; on the deck sat a young man and a woman.

Mike came about, made a slow approach into the wind. Luke stood on the foredeck and called across the water: "Hello aboard the *Viviane*. When did the *Dorado* leave?"

"Late yesterday: three or four o'clock."

The trimaran edged slowly closer, and drifted as Mike eased the sheets. Luke asked, "Any idea where they were bound for?"

"Hiva Oa, according to the skipper. Then Tahiti."

"Would you know what particular place on Hiva Oa?"

"We just came up from Hana Menu: that's a bay on the north coast: very beautiful! I mentioned it to the people on the *Dorado*; I think they might be putting in there."

"Thank you!"

Luke turned to the Australians. "How much to sail me to Hiva Oa?"

"Well, let's consider," said Mike. "That's about sixty miles, give or take a bit. It's on the way to Tahiti. Bob, have you had enough of Nuku Hiva?"

"I'm ready for Hiva Oa."

"Right. Well, then: say thirty dollars. Why so cheap? We're lonesome and crave company. Also we're short of funds."

The *Banshee* put out of Tai Oa Bay, tacking into the southeast trades which suddenly had come to life. Hiva Oa lay dead southeast, and unless the wind shifted the trip would be a thrash into head-winds.

The seas began to mount. The Australians furled the mainsail and continued under jib and mizzen with some small diminution of speed and a far easier motion.

During the afternoon Hiva Oa became visible: a long black outline marked by the twin mountains Heani and Ootua.

The wind lessened, and it became apparent that the trimaran would not reach Hiva Oa by nightfall. The breeze became fitful; clouds began to gather in the east; a squall was imminent. At sunset, with the sky a weird muddle of hurrying clouds, the Australians hove to under the mizzen. With the first gust of wind and rain, all went below.

In the cabin there was quiet except for the gentle surge of water against the hull. The boat moved easily, rolling not at all, rising and falling with a gentler motion than Luke had experienced on the *Rahiria*. When he slid back the hatch and raised his head to see what was going on topside, the wind whistled past his ears, raindrops stung his face. He quickly returned below. "Are we moving ahead or astern?"

"About holding our own, I fancy," Mike told him. "Maybe we'll be blown back five miles or so. Maybe we'll draw ahead a little. Nothing to fear." He glanced at the chart. "Ua Pu is thirty miles west, ample under the circumstances. We're right as rain."

Dinner was soup, bread, fruit, canned meat stewed with potatoes and onions: much the same fare Luke had enjoyed on the *Rahiria*.

After the meal, Bob went up on deck, Mike washed dishes, Luke sat brooding on the settee. Bob returned below with cheerful news. "Weather's breaking up; she'll be calm the rest of the night. Might as well all turn in."

Mike and Bob slept in the wing bunks; Luke spent what he believed to be a fitful night on the settee, but before he knew it the light of dawn was flooding the cabin. He roused himself, pulled on his shoes, went out on deck. The day was clear; the wind gentle, but still from the southeast. Ahead lay Hiva Oa, at about the same distance as on the previous evening.

Mike came on deck, raised jib and mainsail, set the wind-vane which automatically steered the boat. Bob made coffee and boiled oatmeal. "If conditions keep like this," said Mike, "we'll make Hiva Oa by noon. A beastly trip, of course. With anything like a fair wind we'd do sixty miles in three or four hours."

The sun rose into a sky of the purest blue; the wind lessened, the trimaran lazed through clear blue water.

Luke went to sit on the forward part of the cabin with binoculars, peering toward Hiva Oa, in dread lest he spy the *Dorado* with all sails set faring to the south. It was a wonderful morning. He thought with regret how much he might have enjoyed such a sail had circumstances been different…

The morning wore on. The *Banshee* moved at a leisurely pace toward the island. The peaks lifted into the sky; the terminal capes extended across the horizon; the blacks and grays began to reveal shades of green.

After consulting the chart, Mike set a course directly toward Mount Heani, and presently the two juts of rock enclosing Hana Menu became visible.

Beyond, dividing the bay into an eastern and western cove, stood an enormous tower of rock, which Bob announced to be seven hundred feet high.

Exactly at noon the *Banshee* entered Hana Menu. In the eastern bight were two vessels. The first was the *Rahiria*, tied up at a dock; the second, to Luke's inexpressible relief, was the *Dorado*, at anchor two hundred yards off a fine white beach, and almost in the shadow of the great tower.

"Well, matey, looks like you're in luck," said Mike. "There's your boat at last."

"There she is indeed," said Luke. "Put me alongside, if you will."

"Ten dollars if you please: fare from Taio Hae to Tai Oa. Another thirty, passage from Tai Oa to Hana Menu."

Luke found his traveler's checks, signed his name. "Here's fifty. Buy a beer when you reach Papeete."

"That we will, and much obliged."

"Much obliged to you."

The trimaran approached the *Dorado*. Mike said, "There's nobody aboard. Looks to me like they're all ashore."

Luke took the binoculars, and indeed the *Dorado* appeared to be deserted. Where was everybody? He scanned the shore. At the end of the bay was a village, picturesque under cocoanut palms. Some sort of celebration seemed to be in progress. Smoke from a number of fires drifted up through the trees; light-colored garments flickered in the shade.

Bob studied the scene through the binoculars. "Looks like a big *tamaraa*. Maybe we should stay over."

"We're not invited, Bob my boy. It's Papeete for us."

"You're making a mistake, Hannigan. Remember those gorgeous dollies aboard the *Dorado*?"

"I also saw a couple of hard-looking Yanks, not to mention that chap we ferried aboard. Seems to me he got the glad-eye from one of them."

"You're right," said Bob. "Noticed it myself. The one who was on the lookout for him."

Luke was immediately interested. "Which one was that?"

"Hard to describe, matey. They had a great deal in common."

"Careful, Mike! Maybe one was Luke's sister?"

"No," said Luke. "Nothing like that…Well, put me ashore, if you will. That's where everybody seems to be."

"Just as you say."

The trimaran slid up to the dock; Luke jumped ashore and Mike handed up his suitcase. On the beach appeared a girl in white shorts and a pale blue halter. Bob snatched up the binoculars. "Oh, you beauty! You wonderful specimen!"

"Here! Let me look." Mike seized the binoculars, but the girl had already turned back under the trees.

"Who was it?" asked Luke anxiously. "The one who gave the 'glad-eye' to Easley?"

"Can't be all that certain; she was walking away from me. The other had her hair in a tuft, or so I recollect. I'd wanter see more of her than just her backside."

Mike snorted. "Never satisfied, that's Bob Higgins for you."

"I said I couldn't make no good identification of just her backside!"

"Nothing wrong with that either."

"Well then. Kick us off, Luke, we'll be putting to sea."

Luke obliged. The sails bellied, the *Banshee* leaned upon its lee float and slid away toward the ocean.

Luke took his suitcase and set off down the dock, past the *Rahiria*, then along the road beside the bay. Ironwood trees, an occasional mango, the ever-present cocoanut palms overhung the road. Thatch huts stood a few yards back in the shade.

Luke pondered as he walked. If Brady was attending a feast on the beach, he could not know that Carson was dead. Luke made his plans. By one means or another he would signal Brady away from the party, break the bad news and reveal what he knew about Easley. The identity of Easley's accomplice — Lia? Jean Wintersea? Kelsey McClure? — could not be concealed. The whole sorry mess must be illuminated, for better or worse.

Luke passed through the little village with its inevitable church and Chinese grocery, and approached the *tamaraa*: a feast obviously commissioned by Brady. Food was heaped on four tables: steamed pork and chicken; crayfish, raw fish in lime juice, *langouste*, fried fish, fish balls in cocoanut cream, three kinds of poi, rice, bananas, papaya, avocados, minced clams in fermented cocoanut curd, heart of palm, octopus stewed in its own ink, a custard of canned milk flavored with vanilla bean and coffee.

It appeared that the company from the *Dorado* had already eaten. Now they sat drinking wine and watching dancers from the village.

Halting back in the shadows, Luke studied the people present. Brady was invisible; Easley was nowhere to be seen; no one fit his mental picture of Lia. With the exception of Bill Sarvis, the *Dorado's* Chief Engineer, the persons at the *tamaraa* were strangers.

Sarvis, now sixty years old, was a man not too tall, pale for a seaman, with a face all bone and cartilage. Luke tossed a pebble at Sarvis, who looked around. Luke signaled. Sarvis rose to his feet, ambled across the clearing. "Hello, Luke. Thought we were to meet you in Nuku Hiva."

"That was my idea too. I was delayed. By the time I found out where the *Dorado* was anchored, you'd already set sail."

Sarvis scowled, rubbed his chin. "Strange. The skipper got word that you weren't aboard the schooner."

"For reasons I can't explain right now, I used another name: Jim Harrison. Does Brady know that Carson drowned?"

"What? You don't mean it?"

"I certainly do. On the way up from Tahiti."

"My lord no. What a terrible thing! Poor Brady! He left the kid in Honolulu. Well, I guess you know about that. How did it happen?"

"Something of a mystery. Where is Brady?"

"He took sick, ate something which didn't agree with him. He and the missus went back aboard the *Dorado.*"

Luke stared at Sarvis, then at the loaded tables, then out toward the *Dorado.* "What made him sick?"

Sarvis shrugged. "Hard to say. Whatever it was he didn't like it."

Luke drew a long deep breath. Had Easley been at work so swiftly?

He heard a footfall, and there, as if summoned by Luke's conjectures, stood Easley. "Hi, there, Harrison," said Easley, without enthusiasm. "What brings you here?"

"I might ask the same of you."

Easley waited a moment before replying, an insulting pause, as if Luke's question deserved no instant response. "I'm a guest aboard the *Dorado.*" He jerked his head toward the *Rahiria.* "You'd better get aboard or you'll be marooned. They're about ready to cast off."

Luke opened his mouth, then shut it. Let Easley think he had arrived aboard the *Rahiria.*

"How come you didn't tell Mr. Royce that his son was drowned?"

"Who? Carson?" Easley wore an expression of surprise. "Was he Royce's son? I don't believe I ever heard his last name."

Luke turned to Sarvis. "Take me out to the *Dorado*. I'll have to tell Mr. Royce what's happened."

Easley looked toward the *Rahiria*, which indeed was on the verge of departure, then shrugged and walked away.

Luke said, "That man is the reason I'm calling myself Jim Harrison."

"I've been wondering," said Sarvis.

"Well, it's my name until I tell you otherwise. Let's go out and give Brady the news."

"Come along then. The launch is this way."

A few minutes later they nosed in under the *Dorado*'s accommodation ladder. Luke climbed aboard. The decks were vacant. He looked into the main saloon, to find a Filipino steward wiping down the brass work.

"Where's Mr. Royce?"

"He's in his stateroom. Pretty sick."

"Mrs. Royce is with him?"

"Yes sir."

"Go ask if I can speak to him."

The steward went aft. A moment later a dark-haired young woman with a pale olive skin appeared in the saloon. She wore white shorts, a pullover blouse of beige cotton, and Luke was forced to admit that Lia Wintersea Royce was far and away the most beautiful creature he had ever seen face to face. At the moment she appeared nervous and on the verge of tears. "Yes? What do you want?" Her voice was gentle; her brusqueness was not intended to give offense.

"I'd like to see Mr. Royce."

Lia jerked out her hands. "I don't see how you can just now. He's terribly sick."

"How sick?"

"Well, he's vomiting. He has stomach cramps and — he's really not himself."

"You've called for a doctor?"

"Of course. There's a hospital down the shore; the doctor should be here at once. Who are you?"

Luke evaded the question. "Does Mr. Royce know that his son Carson is dead?"

Lia blinked, drew back and became ghostly pale. "Carson? Dead?"

Luke nodded grimly. If Lia was acting, her performance was superb.

"He drowned on the way up from Tahiti. Apparently he fell overboard."

"How perfectly awful," whispered Lia to herself. She looked uncertainly down the passageway. "I can't tell Brady. I simply can't tell him now. He's so miserable..."

"May I see him a moment or two?"

Lia searched his face with as much concentration as she seemed able to summon. "You're a friend of his?"

"That's about it."

"I really don't think you should. Not right now. I should be with him...Thank God! Here's the doctor!"

A young man in white trousers and a white shirt came into the saloon, carrying a professional black bag. He asked questions in barely accented English, and Lia, ignoring Luke, took him aft to the stateroom.

Luke turned to Sarvis. "Well, that's that."

"What's going on, if you don't mind my asking?" Sarvis asked.

"I don't mind. I believe that Easley knocked Carson on the head and threw him overboard. In Tahiti he tried to kill me. I was wearing a beard then; now he doesn't recognize me. He's a murderer — but I can't prove it. I tried to get here, to talk to Brady, but it looks like I'm late."

Sarvis' eyes jerked open wide. "You don't mean —"

"I don't know. It's strange that no one else is sick. Just Brady."

"Strange for a fact." Sarvis rubbed his chin, producing a grating noise.

Luke went out on deck and looked toward shore. The sound of music and singing drifted across the water; the *tamaraa* was a great success. The *Rahiria* had departed, the *Dorado* was the only yacht in the bay.

Fifteen minutes passed. Luke returned to the saloon. Sarvis sat brooding.

Luke paced back and forth.

The doctor appeared, followed by Lia, who was biting her lips.

Luke asked, "How is he?"

The doctor set his bag on the table. "Frankly, he's not well." He spoke in a precise voice. "I believe that he has eaten poison fish. There are many kinds of poison fish. Some become toxic from the waters where they live, the food they eat. A parrot fish caught here is safe, a parrot fish caught ten kilometers around the island is toxic... But these are not so dangerous. A person may become very sick. But usually he recovers. If Mr. Royce has eaten what the natives call *hue-hue* — that is to say, puffer fish — then the situation is more critical."

"I see. Well — what do you think?"

"I can't be sure. The symptoms are in many cases the same: vomiting, diarrhea, convulsions, loss of sensation in the extremities. I've done what I can for him. We can only hope for the best. Additionally, Mr. Royce seems to have a history of liver trouble which complicates matters." He picked up his bag. "No one else is sick?"

Sarvis replied, "No one that we know of."

"Strange... The natives won't catch *hue-hue*; they're afraid of it. Although if the gland is removed it's quite safe." He shrugged, turned to Lia. "I must go ashore, but I'll be back in two hours."

"Shouldn't we move him to the hospital?" quavered Lia.

"It would do no good. I can't do anything there I can't do here. In Papeete they might do better. If you wish I'll radio for the seaplane. Naturally there is expense."

"Don't mind the expense! Radio for the seaplane!"

"Very well. In the meantime, see that he's quiet. Let him rest as much as possible." The doctor departed; a moment later his launch surged past and away toward shore.

Luke flung himself down on the settee and stared at the carpet. Lia went back along the passageway. Sarvis came to stand in front of Luke. "You think Easley is responsible for this?"

"I know he is."

"Why?" asked Sarvis evenly. "What for? For whose benefit?"

"Figure it out for yourself."

"The way things stand, you'd be the only one to benefit."

Luke raised his head, met Sarvis' cool grey gaze. "Easley tried to kill me first. He thought he had succeeded. I was riding a motor-scooter; he drove me over a cliff. He thinks I'm dead."

"If he had known you were alive, he might not have killed Carson. If, in fact, he did so."

"That's true," said Luke. "But I knew nothing of his intentions. If he's responsible for this —" Luke nodded toward the aft stateroom "— then things start to take shape."

Sarvis grunted. "If Brady dies, it's your word against his."

"Just one matter," said Luke. "How am I supposed to have poisoned Brady?"

"You had as much chance as Easley had. The *Rahiria* has been in port since last night."

Luke grinned. "I see. Well, Sarvis, you suspect whomever you like. But for now — until things straighten out — I'm Jim Harrison. Remember that!"

"Whatever you say. I think I'd better pick up the folk ashore."

"Bring my suitcase over, will you? I left it near where we were talking."

"Right."

Sarvis presently returned with a load of subdued guests. Sarvis tersely introduced Luke as 'Mr. Harrison', which seemed to suffice for the moment. Easley, coming into the saloon, stared thoughtfully at Luke, then went off to his stateroom.

Lia emerged. In a hushed voice she reported the doctor's diagnosis, and then she began to sob. Luke watched her carefully, and the other two young women as well. If Lia was acting, thought Luke, her technique was beyond reproach.

The other two? He was able to form no immediate opinion. Both were formally sympathetic; neither gave evidence of deep concern. Jean was cool and didactic: her emotions were carefully intellectualized. Kelsey, saucy, spoiled, effervescent with mischief, clearly intended to waste no concern on troubles not her own. A fascinating little creature, thought Luke — more vital and self-aware than Lia, more feminine than Jean, and already appraising Luke, the new man aboard. Luke refused to respond. She was quite possibly a murderess — more properly, a murderer's accomplice, but why boggle at the distinction? The word almost certainly fitted one of the three young women aboard the *Dorado*.

Which?

Simple inspection yielded no information.

The other guests Luke dismissed with a cursory inspection. Don Peppergold seemed a straightforward young man if somewhat bumptious. The older McClures could not possibly be anything but what they seemed to be: a prosperous middle-aged couple, civilized, intelligent, decent by long habit rather than conscious doctrine. Easley was alien to the group: at least to the older McClures and to Don Peppergold. Luke heard Kelsey call him "Ben" and Jean for a period sat with him in the corner of the saloon.

The doctor returned and without words went into the stateroom. Lia came into the saloon, to stand troubled and alone.

Conversation halted. The steward brought tea, which was sipped in near-silence. Everyone ignored Luke.

The doctor appeared briefly. "I radioed for the seaplane," he told Lia. "It is probably the best we can do for Mr. Royce, to get him to Papeete. They have new techniques and drugs which so far are not available to us."

"When will the seaplane arrive?"

"I can't be sure. Certainly within an hour or two. There will be trained attendants aboard; I have seen to that."

"Thank you very much."

The doctor returned to the aft stateroom. Lia sat down and listlessly sipped the tea which Mrs. McClure forced upon her. Whatever her thoughts, she kept them to herself, with only jerks and twitches of her mouth to indicate that she was thinking at all.

Luke leaned back on the settee, watching everyone through half-closed eyes. No one seemed to heed him except possibly Easley, who from time to time turned him a brooding glance of speculation.

The doctor emerged from the stateroom. He looked haggard, dismayed, a trifle bewildered, as if he too found the events confusing. Without preamble, without so much as clearing his throat he announced: "Mr. Royce has passed away."

Silence held the air. Lia gave a little moan and fell to sobbing against Mrs. McClure. Easley reached for a cigar but thought better of it. Luke watched to see with whom, if anyone, he would exchange a glance of triumph.

Jean sat with her mouth pinched, her forehead creased, as if she were worried. Kelsey watched Lia with an unreadable expression.

Luke met the gaze of William Sarvis. He knew what Sarvis was thinking: the obvious; what else? He, Luke Royce, was now administrator of the Golconda Fund, a *de facto* millionaire, master of enormous wealth. The *Dorado*, which heaved on the easy swells of Hana Menu, was his. Beautiful women, as beautiful as Lia, were at his command. He was now a powerful man. Luke gave a wry grimace, trying to drive the thoughts from his mind. For a fact, they held no pleasure. The only reality was here in the saloon of the *Dorado*. The murderer was known; who was the murderess? Luke looked from face to face: from Lia to Jean to Kelsey. The doctor was talking in tense hurried tones to Lia, who listened numbly, nodding from time to time, her beautiful eyes glinting with tears. Jean watched with a detached frowning interest. Now she darted a quick glance toward Easley. So far as Luke could determine it seemed exploratory, questioning, rather than communicative. Easley was making bored O's with his mouth, smoking a non-existent cigar. Kelsey? She appeared resentful, as if Brady's death were a tiresome and inconsiderate act.

Lia? Jean? Kelsey? One must be guilty; one of these had brought Easley to the *Dorado*; either Lia or Jean or Kelsey had plotted with Easley to kill three men.

Two were dead; one remained alive. Easley and someone unnamed were about to receive a terrible shock.

Luke looked again toward Sarvis. The cold gray eyes no longer probed him. Instead they were fixed upon Ben Easley. By some unconscious device, Luke had convinced William Sarvis of his innocence.

Luke pulled himself upright on the settee. It was a time for plans. Easley and his accomplice would not casually reveal themselves. Their guilt had to be demonstrated. At the moment Luke could invent no method to compel such a demonstration.

Chapter XVIII

The seaplane arrived at seven o'clock, skimming low across the dusky bay, settling in a fan of spray.

The district gendarme had already been aboard and had conferred with the doctor. He manifestly felt out of his depth; he stated that he would investigate the circumstances at the *tamaraa* and report to the Papeete authorities, which would be to the convenience of all, since the *Dorado* was bound there in any case.

Brady's body was transferred to the seaplane.

Lia declared her intention of accompanying the body to Papeete. The McClures argued against this course, pointing out that she could effect nothing meaningful at Papeete, that for the time she was better off aboard the *Dorado* in the company of her friends.

Lia listened dubiously. "But I should get in touch with Luke Royce — after all, he's the new administrator of the estate."

Jean joined the conversation. "Send him a radio message. A few days won't mean anything to him."

Lia turned to Sarvis. "What do you think?"

"We'll be in Papeete inside of four days, if we hoist anchor right now. We can certainly send a radiogram to Luke Royce at his Papeete address."

"Very well then," said Lia in a wan voice. "Can we sail right now?"

"Certainly, ma'am."

Lia turned wearily away. As she passed Easley he stopped her, muttered a sentence or two. Lia turned a puzzled gaze toward Luke, and hesitated. Then she turned back. "I'm sorry, but I don't quite understand why you're aboard."

Luke had been expecting some such challenge; indeed for the last few minutes he had been receiving dubious glances from everyone in the saloon.

He responded carefully, aware that everyone was watching and listening. "I came up from Tahiti aboard the *Rahiria*, as perhaps Mr. Easley has told you."

"'Easley'?" Lia looked around in puzzlement. "You mean Ben? His name isn't Easley." She looked toward Ben Eiselhardt, who merely grinned and fished in his pocket for a cigar.

"Whatever he chooses to call himself," said Luke, "he and I and Carson were all aboard the *Rahiria*. I came aboard the *Dorado* to speak to Brady Royce, and while I was here the *Rahiria* sailed."

Ben Eiselhardt spoke in an offhand voice. "And now the *Dorado* is about to sail. It's time you were going ashore."

Luke paid him no heed, and continued to address Lia. "I hoped to presume upon your good nature for transportation back to Tahiti."

Lia gazed at him numbly, not wanting a stranger aboard, but unwilling to seem ungracious. She looked helplessly toward Malcolm McClure, who cleared his throat. "I think, sir, that under these tragic conditions —"

Luke rose to his feet. He addressed Lia. "May I speak to you privately?"

Lia took him out on deck. "Well?"

Luke sighed. To reveal his identity even to one of his suspects was a pity — but now a necessity. Lia had been on the point of ordering him off the ship.

Luke looked around to make sure that he could not be overheard. "You've never met me. I'm Luke Royce."

"You're Luke Royce!" Lia raised her hand to her neck, peered at him. "I thought your name was Harrison, or something of the sort!"

"For reasons I won't go into now, I called myself Harrison. But I'm Luke Royce. Bill Sarvis knows me well. If you don't believe me, ask him. Or I can show you my passport."

"I believe you — but why...There's so much I don't understand."

"There's a great deal I don't understand either. I came aboard hoping to discuss the situation with Brady. But — as you know —"

"Yes. I know. Well — I can't very well order you from the boat. It's actually your boat."

"I'd like you not to tell anyone who I am. I want to —"

"No," cried Lia, in a strange desperate voice. "I won't have any more mystery! I can't stand any more! Come back into the saloon. Naturally you can stay aboard. But everyone must know who you are."

"Oh very well," said Luke. "It doesn't make all that difference."

Lia marched back into the saloon, with Luke coming behind, feeling a trifle sheepish.

Lia spoke in a voice so sharp as almost to be strident: "This man's name is not Harrison. He tells me that he is Luke Royce. He owns the boat. We are all his guests, not the other way around."

Luke was desperately trying to watch three faces at once, those of Easley, Jean Wintersea, Kelsey McClure. All three faces changed. Easley's face suddenly lost its cool bravado, and for a stricken instant became the face of a little boy. His eyes glistened — with tears? He turned abruptly away, went to look out a porthole. Luke could understand his frustration. The totality of his hopes, the entire cast of his plans, lay in ruins. What he had striven to achieve was totally lost; he had strained and worked and killed for nothing.

Jean's face altered by no twitch of a muscle. But an internal change occurred, or perhaps this was Luke's imagination. Her head seemed to be all skull, with the finest membrane of skin stretched over bare bone, with hollow pits for eyes. Kelsey's surprise was less controlled. Her jaw dropped; her eyes seemed to bulge and where Jean had grown pale, Kelsey suddenly flushed.

Reactions there were, beyond dispute. But how to interpret them? And what of Lia? He had spoken to her in the semi-darkness, he had not been able to study her as closely as he might have wished. She had evinced natural surprise, together with a trace of equally normal resentment. Still, if Lia were in fact Ben Eiselhardt's accomplice, she already had demonstrated an ability to dissemble far beyond the ordinary. Luke looked back to Easley — he must start thinking of him as Eiselhardt — hoping to observe an exchange of glances with someone, when he finally turned away from the porthole.

The silence persisted a moment or two, with everybody uncertain how to meet the new situation. Malcolm McClure said at last, in a stifled voice, "I won't pretend that I understand any of this, but I suppose the least we can do —" he changed to a tone of facetious irony "— is make you welcome to the group."

"What are your orders, Mr. Royce?" Bill Sarvis asked in a quiet voice.

"Just as before. We'll proceed to Papeete."

Don Peppergold had been standing back, head skeptically cocked, giving Luke a careful inspection. "Just for the record," he said, "may I look at your passport?"

"Certainly." Luke produced the document. Don Peppergold studied it. Malcolm McClure came to look over his shoulder; Ben Eiselhardt made a similar move, then checked himself. He looked toward Luke, and for an instant Luke met his gaze. It was so full of dreadful meaning that Luke felt sick. Ben Eiselhardt's first attempt on his life had been a casual act upon which Eiselhardt had spent no emotion. Eiselhardt would try again, as an act of passion. Emotion bloated him, distended his mouth, affected the pitch of his voice. Never in his life had Ben Eiselhardt been so frustrated.

Don Peppergold returned the passport with a faint shrug. Lia had been watching with poorly disguised hope. Her face sagged. She turned to Luke. "I'll move out of the owner's stateroom; you can move in."

"Of course not," said Luke. "Don't inconvenience yourself in any way. I'll be happy anywhere. Just carry on as before."

Lia thought a moment. Then she said, "Jean will move in with me, and you can have her cabin."

"That suits me very well," said Luke.

Sarvis caught his eye. "Shall we heave anchor?"

Luke nodded. "I don't imagine any of us wants to prolong the cruise. At Papeete whoever wishes can fly back to the States."

Sarvis departed; others in the group went off to their staterooms, Jean to move her belongings, others to change clothes. McClure and Peppergold muttered together, and presently both approached Luke.

"Sorry to be persistent, Mr. Royce," said McClure, "but Don and I are profoundly disturbed by the situation. First Carson dies, then Brady. You are the obvious beneficiary. Mind you, we make no accusations; we merely want to bring the situation out into the open."

"Quite all right," said Luke. "I understand your doubts. There'll be an investigation as soon as we reach Papeete. I'm sure that the facts of the case will emerge."

Peppergold thrust his face pugnaciously forward, stimulating himself into a state of artificial and unconvincing zeal. "You don't intend to explain why you used a false name?"

"No, I don't," said Luke. "I had a good reason."

"I'm afraid I can't be satisfied with that."

"Let's not jump to conclusions," said McClure in a reasonable voice. "As Mr. Royce points out, there's sure to be an investigation at Papeete. Mr. Royce doesn't appear to worry about this, so I think we ought to defer judgment."

Peppergold shook his head, turned away and left the saloon. "He's an attorney," McClure told Luke. "He wants everything in black and white, cut and dried. An impatient fellow, perhaps a trifle bull-headed. I've no doubt that he'll be a great success."

"And what about you? How do you feel?"

McClure smiled. "I'm uncommitted — for now. I think I can guess what's at the back of your mind. If I'm correct, you naturally don't want to tip your hand."

"Close enough," said Luke. "Well, I'd better have a word with Sarvis. I've crewed aboard this ship, but I'm no navigator. If we steer southwest for about three days, and don't run aground in the Tuamotus, I imagine we can home into Papeete by radio direction-finder."

"As good a system as any," said McClure. "As a matter of fact, I'm a navigator. If you'll allow me, I'll take charge of that end of it."

"Please do."

CHAPTER XIX

THE NEXT MORNING found the *Dorado* cruising across a sparkling blue sea, flying fish skipping away to either side.

Lia and Jean appeared for breakfast, both reserved and thoughtful. Lia made a wan effort to be gracious; Jean brooded through the entire meal, her face a mask.

Luke found the company's mood even chillier than on the previous evening, as if, after reflection, all had decided Luke to be an unfeeling interloper — if nothing worse. Luke ate his breakfast with equanimity. From the corner of his eye he saw Easley studying him, a wistful droop to his mouth.

After breakfast Luke found Sarvis and took him aft to the taffrail. "Well, Bill," said Luke, "you've slept on the situation. What do you make of it now?"

"I think what I thought yesterday," said Sarvis. "There's something dreadful going on."

"I'll tell you the rest of the story." Luke described his initial encounter with Ben Eiselhardt. "If everything had worked out as planned, Mrs. Royce would now be sole administrator to the Fund. This must be the motivating force behind the affair."

"What would she gain?" demanded Sarvis. "Brady gave her everything she wanted. Why risk any of it?"

"People do strange things," said Luke. "But perhaps she's not responsible at all. It might be Jean Wintersea or Kelsey. How would one of these profit? She'd have to know that she could control Lia; Eiselhardt would also have to be certain. He wouldn't work for nothing… Here's Lia now, she's got something on her mind."

Lia came slowly aft. "May I join you?"

"Certainly," said Luke. "In fact, there's a question I want to ask you."

Lia instantly became wary, and looked as if she wished she had stayed away.

"Sarvis and I are wondering how Mr. Eiselhardt comes to be aboard the *Dorado*. Was he a friend of Brady's?"

"Oh no, nothing like that." Lia compressed her lips and looked aft down the line of wake. "I knew him long ago — when I was in high school in fact. In Nuku Hiva he heard the *Dorado* was nearby and came to visit. I was naturally surprised, and invited him aboard. It's as simple as that."

"Brady didn't object?"

Lia shrugged. "I don't think he cared much, one way or the other."

"They were strangers?"

"Oh yes. But Brady was very generous. Why are you asking these questions?"

"Curiosity," said Luke. "They are questions the police are sure to ask."

Lia nodded slowly. "That's what I came to talk to you about: the police. Do you think there will be an investigation?"

"I'm sure of it."

"I've been wondering — well, why can't it be avoided? Brady's death was a tragic accident — but certainly an accident. Wouldn't it be best to minimize the situation? People can be so cruel."

"Whose idea is this?" asked Sarvis. "Your own? Or have you been advised by others?"

Lia flushed. "It's partly my own idea. I've naturally discussed the matter with other people."

"Who, for instance?"

"My sister, for one."

Luke shook his head. "We can't avoid a police inquiry, even if we wanted to. The circumstances are very strange, to say the least."

"I suppose you're right." Lia turned away, but halted. "We couldn't just — well, sail directly back to California?"

"I don't think it would be wise, Mrs. Royce."

Lia sighed and once more turned away.

Luke called after her. "One more question, Mrs. Royce. Was your sister previously acquainted with Mr. Eiselhardt?"

"Yes, I suppose so. She was two years ahead of me, in the same class with Ben."

"What about Miss McClure?"

"She was in my class. She knew Ben too, at least by sight. But why are you asking these questions?"

"As before, curiosity. And I'd just as soon you kept our conversation to yourself."

"Oh, certainly. I wouldn't want to disturb anyone." She smiled politely and went forward.

"It's hard to imagine Mrs. Royce guilty of anything — on her own hook," remarked Sarvis.

"No. She seems malleable — but not vicious. Can we get in radio contact with the States?"

"We should be able to raise Honolulu without any trouble. San Francisco if the atmosphere is right."

"I want to send a message right away."

A day passed and a second day, with the *Dorado* sliding closer to Papeete on fair winds. The passengers sat in clusters, talking together with furtive glances up and down the deck. Luke wandered here and there. When he approached one of the groups, voices dwindled away. Meals were even more uncomfortable, with conversation confined to brief unreal spatters, like the dialogue in an amateur theatrical. Lia haunted her cabin, appearing on deck or in the saloon with a wan face and eyes red-rimmed behind dark glasses.

Tension gripped the *Dorado:* knuckle-gnawing stomach-griping anxiety. Luke could feel it, but could not trace its source. Eiselhardt, who should be on tenterhooks, seemed unconcerned. Lia, Jean, Kelsey: all showed signs of edginess. One of the three, by Luke's theories, should feel an almost unbearable foreboding. Nothing of the sort was evident. Luke wondered why. Were the guilty pair so nerveless, so confident of their invulnerability? Or was there some new grimness in the offing? Luke winced and looked over his shoulder. The tension and anxiety quite possibly derived from himself. For instance, if he were to disappear from the ship, if a scrawled note, purportedly in his handwriting, were to be found, the French authorities would not be likely to look farther for a solution. Luke walked with care, looking and listening. He found and took possession of Brady's .38 revolver which seemed to be the only fire-arm aboard.

The *Dorado* entered the Tuamotus. Twice atolls appeared on the horizon like mirages, to move astern and disappear. Luke pondered and watched and wondered. From time to time he became aware of Ben Eiselhardt's puzzled inspection, as if he were wondering who was the bearded man who had been forced over the Teahupoo cliff?

Lia remained numb. She refused to speak to Luke or even look at him. Jean's coolness verged upon hostility. Kelsey's moods were more complex, ranging from an insouciance which annoyed her parents to a bored indifference which provoked and frustrated Don Peppergold. On the afternoon of the third day she came from the saloon and as Don loped forward to meet her she smartly accelerated her pace, dropped into a deck-chair beside Luke. Don glared for a moment, then swung away.

Luke sat in silence, though acutely aware of the shapely brown legs, the turn of hip in the tight white shorts. Kelsey, he suspected, was equally aware of the circumstances.

A minute or two passed, and Kelsey at last spoke. "What a strange man you are!"

"Come now," said Luke. "You know better than that."

"*I* know? How should *I* know?"

"Female instinct."

"That's one way," Kelsey admitted. "But it's not infallible. My mother, for instance, is afraid that an era has passed. You don't impress her as being a true Royce. Not spectacular enough."

"Well — I've never really set my mind to it. What would she think if I marooned her on that atoll out there?"

Kelsey laughed and stretched out her legs. "She'd be outraged. But she'd never again accuse you of being meek and unobtrusive."

" 'Meek and unobtrusive', eh?" Luke glanced sardonically sidewise at Kelsey, who sat with her lips pursed. "Oh well, I guess it's better than being called 'rude and obtrusive'."

"Unfortunately," said Kelsey, "you've aroused criticism along these lines too."

"I never considered myself perfect," said Luke. "Well then — what's your opinion?"

"I'm not saying."

"You knew Brady a long time?"

Kelsey reacted to the change of subject by giving her feet an irritated twitch. "As long as I remember."

"And Lia?"

"Since high school. We were both on rally committee. Pom-pom girls, if you must know the truth. Jean played in the orchestra. Not the marching band. She was a serious-minded teenager."

"And she's changed?"

"She's no longer a teenager, if that's what you mean."

"I don't mean anything in particular. But it's strange to find three beautiful girls being chums."

Kelsey wrinkled her nose. "'Chums' isn't quite the word. Close enough, I suppose. They lived in a very odd household, very musical, very intense. Lia upset everyone, being tone-deaf, and I used to fear for her morale."

"What about Eiselhardt?"

"There he is. He exists."

"You knew him in high school too?"

"I knew who he was. We moved in different circles."

Don Peppergold could restrain himself no longer. He sauntered past, halted as if in surprise. "Hi there, girl. How about a game of cribbage to break the monotony?"

"No thanks."

"But it's three o'clock!"

"Go try Mother. She's a lot better player than I am."

Don Peppergold departed. Five minutes later Dorothy McClure emerged from the saloon and called Kelsey in a faintly scandalized voice. "Don is such a tattle-tale," said Kelsey. "Oh well…" She hoisted herself to her feet and strolled off to the saloon. With tremendous effort Luke restrained himself from looking after her. From the corner of his eye he noticed that as Kelsey swung down the companionway she flashed a glance toward him over her shoulder.

The voyage proceeded. Luke's suspicions inclined first this way, then that. In the strictest sense, Dorothy McClure should also be considered a suspect, Luke told himself. She was slender and small and almost as well-shaped as her daughter, though here the similarity ended...Luke brought his imagination under control. The idea of Dorothy McClure as the accomplice of Ben Eiselhardt was too weird to be entertained. Still, stranger things had happened.

The Tuamotus lay astern. At sunset of the fourth day clouds piled up in the west: towers of gold looking westward over a vermilion skyscape: sheer exaltation. Dinner this particular evening was a strange affair, with everyone in a state of hyperaesthesia, so that the most minute signals took on extravagant meanings. The situation had reached a stage where a touch, a jolt, a word, might easily set off someone's screaming hysteria. Sarvis alone seemed steady, a rock of normalcy.

"Tomorrow, about noon," said Malcolm McClure, "we should have landfall, and be into port by two or three."

"What a relief," murmured Dorothy McClure. "With Brady dead, it's been such a desolate ship."

Malcolm McClure gave a noncommittal grunt. "A pleasure, certainly, to put all this behind us."

Lia asked gingerly, "And there will really be an investigation? By the police?"

"I should imagine so," said Malcolm McClure curtly.

"There'll be an investigation," said Luke.

"But —" Lia started to speak then became silent.

Dorothy McClure said somewhat nervously: "Surely they'll understand that the whole thing was a ghastly accident, a mistake on somebody's part."

"Unfortunately," said Sarvis, "the circumstances suggest something worse. Not an accident. Not a mistake."

"But that would be — murder!"

The word had a peculiar resonance. To Luke's knowledge no one had used it before.

"Yes," said Sarvis. "Murder."

Dorothy McClure made a sound — a girlish titter — which was quite out of character. "I suppose I've lived a sheltered life. Of course, there was that other girl, what was her name?"

"Inez," said Jean flatly. "Inez Gallegos."

"Yes, of course. She seemed so pleasant. Why would anyone want to do such a wicked thing?"

Lia screamed. Everyone looked at her startled. The scene was like an unkind flashlight photograph: Lia leaning back, eyes bulging, mouth open, tongue displayed. She screamed again. "Why do you all torture me?" She fell awkwardly to the deck, picked herself up and half-ran and half-limped from the saloon.

Jean followed her. The sound of muffled sobbing came from the after stateroom.

The night was dark. The *Dorado* hissed through the water. Luke sat on his bunk, fully dressed.

There came a scratching on the panel of his door. The knob turned, the door strained against the lock.

Luke rose to his feet, went to the door. "Who's there?"

A husky female voice said, "Let me in. I want to talk to you."

Luke strained to hear. "Who is it?"

"Open the door, before someone sees me."

"But who is it?"

"Quick! Open the door and you'll see."

"Just a minute." Luke backed away, took up Brady's revolver, cocked it. He went slowly to the door. His hand was trembling. He backed away, sweating. He was afraid to open the door, afraid of what he might see.

There was a stir from somewhere: a door opening, hasty footsteps. Cursing himself for his hesitation, Luke threw open the door, revolver extended toward the opening.

He saw nothing.

Along the passageway, bound for the head, came Malcolm McClure. Luke put the revolver behind his back. McClure nodded, gave a grunt, walked by. Luke said, "I thought I heard someone in the passage. Did you see anyone?"

"One of the girls coming back from the head."

"Oh. Which one?"

"Didn't notice." McClure's eyes glinted as he surveyed Luke head to toe. "Why do you ask?"

"Just general vigilance. This is a nervous ship."

"I'll agree to that." McClure continued down the passage. Luke stood with his door open a crack, waiting, listening. McClure returned to his cabin. Luke eased the door close as he passed and opened it a crack once more, to stand looking out into the passageway.

Water rushed under the hull: a soothing rustle. From somewhere above came the creak of rigging. Otherwise the ship was quiet. But somewhere, two persons lay sweating. Eiselhardt shared a cabin with Don Peppergold, which would handicap Eiselhardt to some extent. Jean and Lia were together; Kelsey was alone.

Luke stood half an hour, but no one returned into the passageway. Who had come to his door? The voice had been a barely audible murmur; it could have been anyone. And why? There seemed three possibilities: to dally, to talk, to kill. The first seemed remote, as did the second. Anyone who wanted to talk could do so by daylight. Luke grimaced and tightened his grip on the revolver. Another ten minutes passed. The *Dorado* was silent. In the saloon the ship's clock sounded eight bells: midnight. There were distant footsteps as the watch changed.

Luke considered going up into the saloon. A dozen eventualities he had not considered: for instance, suppose Eiselhardt... A dreadful thought came to Luke. Caution forgotten he pushed out into the passageway, ran forward to Sarvis' cabin. He knocked. No response. He knocked again, then tried the door, thrust it open. He switched on the light, fearful of what he might see. No Sarvis.

Luke went to McClure's door, rapped. "Open up, McClure; it's Royce."

McClure appeared, belting his dressing gown. "What's the trouble?"

"I don't know. Probably nothing. But come with me please; I need your help."

McClure stepped out into the passage. At the sight of the revolver he scowled. "Why the artillery?"

"Do I have to draw you a picture?" demanded Luke. "Right now I want to find Sarvis; his cabin's empty. I don't want to look alone for fear of someone jumping on my back."

"Very well. But I don't know what you're worried about."

They looked into the saloon. No Sarvis. Luke called out to the man at the wheel. "Anyone out on deck besides you?"

"No, sir."

"Let's try the engine room," said Luke.

The engine room was locked. Luke pounded. "Anyone inside?"

Sarvis' voice came from within. "Who is it?"

"Royce and McClure."

"Are you there, McClure?" asked Sarvis.

"Yes," grumbled McClure. "I'm here."

The door opened, to reveal the grizzled face of the chief engineer.

"I'm not suspicious," said Sarvis. "I just don't believe in taking chances."

"Perhaps I'm a dunce," said McClure, "but why all this to-do?"

"The sea-cocks," said Sarvis. "They're down here in the engine room. Someone might prefer taking his chances in the boats."

"What a dreadful idea," said McClure dubiously.

"I don't like the prospect either," said Sarvis. "That's why I'm here."

CHAPTER XX

THE FAMILIAR HARBOR OPENED in front of the *Dorado*: the sheds and
warehouses of the Quai du Commerce to the left; the old buildings at
the back of storied Quai Bir Hakeim ahead; the new post office, and the
tall flamboyants and ironwood trees to the right. The customs launch
crossed the harbor; the usual set of officials came aboard and with them
a brisk young man in a light gray suit, fresh-faced and limpidly blue of
eye who, in flawless English, introduced himself as Inspector Charles
Duhamel, of the Provincial Gendarmerie. "And who is captain?"

Luke stepped forward. "Since the death of Mr. Brady Royce I have
been acting in that capacity."

"I see. You are — ?"

"Luke Royce."

Duhamel examined Luke more closely. "You are a former resident
of Tahiti?"

"Yes."

"And was there not a circumstance perhaps a month ago —"

"Yes."

Duhamel nodded sagely. "No doubt we will presently find an explanation. I have been in radio communication with the authorities at
both Nuku Hiva and Hiva Oa. The circumstances are such that we may
not avoid a close investigation. I am sure that you all see the necessity
of this." He looked from face to face. "Naturally, no one may leave the
island until we are satisfied that all is in order. We will work with speed,
but inconvenience cannot be avoided. Now, may I ask your names?
And please allow me to glance at your passports. You, sir?"

"I am Malcolm McClure. Here is my passport."

"Thank you, sir." Duhamel made a note of the name. "And you, madame?"

"I am Dorothy McClure."

Duhamel proceeded through the entire group. "Now, may I ask, where you intend to reside during your stay?"

McClure said in a somewhat ponderous voice, "I think that under the circumstances we — myself, my wife and daughter — will stay in a hotel."

Lia looked at Jean. "We will too."

"I'm definitely going ashore," said Don Peppergold.

"Ashore," said Ben Eiselhardt.

"I'll stay aboard," said Luke.

"Very good. All then is decided. The crew no doubt will stay with the ship." Duhamel tapped his teeth with his pencil and looked off across the harbor. "The yacht must of course be moored, and I think that during this time we will begin our inquiries. Mr. McClure, if you please, I will speak with you first. The saloon will be convenient."

Duhamel spoke fifteen minutes with McClure. He spent half an hour with Lia. The *Dorado* meanwhile had backed into the dock, with an anchor holding the bow into the harbor.

Luke was summoned into the saloon next. Duhamel rose to his feet, bowed as Luke entered. "Mr. Royce, please take a seat."

Luke sat down.

"You are the cousin of Mr. Brady Royce?"

"Yes."

"I understand that you traveled to the Marquesas Islands aboard the *Rahiria* and there met the *Dorado.*"

"That's correct."

"Aboard the *Rahiria* was the son of Mr. Royce, who was lost overboard?"

"Yes."

"How do you account for this?"

"I have no certain knowledge of what happened."

"I see. Well, Mr. Royce, let us be frank. I am sure that you realize that we must investigate this matter very carefully."

Luke grinned. "Certainly. I, the apparent beneficiary of the two deaths, am necessarily the prime suspect."

"Naturally!" Duhamel arranged his notebook and pen carefully in front of him, then glanced up sharply at Luke. "What then do you know of the tragic circumstances?"

Luke considered. "I know, or, let us say, I suspect a great deal. I can prove very little. I think that before I tell you what I know and what I suspect — which would take a great deal of time — I would prefer that you interview the other passengers. And then —"

"Ah. But you have definite suspicions?"

"I do. There are one or two matters I want to verify —"

Duhamel held his hand. "Please, Mr. Royce! Allow me to do the investigation. Tell me your suspicions frankly; I will verify or disprove them."

"Just as you say."

"I ask this, you understand, as a formality — are you responsible for these deaths?"

"No."

"I see. And what of your own accident — I now recall some of the circumstances. Were you not reported killed in an accident?"

"This may be the case," said Luke. "The affair occurred just before I left Papeete on the *Rahiria*."

"Why did you not clarify the situation? Your friends must have been distressed."

Luke smiled. "At the time I preferred to be thought dead."

"For a reason connected with our present case?"

"I know now that there is a connection. I didn't then."

Duhamel leaned sharply forward, started to speak, then changed his mind. "Why do you suggest that I interview the others before you describe your suspicions to me?"

"Very simple. I'd like you to acquaint yourself with the persons involved."

"Perhaps this is reasonable. You plan to stay aboard the ship?"

"I'd like to visit the post office."

"I have no objection to this. I think that you had better leave your passport with me."

"I need it to get my mail."

"Yes, of course. A problem. Let me think. There are no airplanes departing until tonight. You may hold your passport. Please return without delay."

Luke nodded. "Thank you."

Luke went ashore, the collective gaze of his erstwhile guests pressing against his back.

The pavement felt strange to his feet: a curious solidity which after days aboard first the *Rahiria*, then the *Dorado*, felt unfamiliar and strange.

He walked along the waterfront toward the post office and almost at once discovered a familiar object: the trimaran *Banshee*. Luke halted, but the decks were empty, the hatches were closed. Mike and Bob were ashore.

Luke continued to the post office, asked for and received his mail. A few personal letters he thrust into his pocket. There was one post-marked the day previously at Papeete. This Luke opened and read:

> Dear Mr. Royce:
>
> According to your instructions I am at the Hotel Tahiti with what material it was possible to accumulate in the time available to me. I fear it will be of no great value.
>
> I await your further instructions,
>
> Sincerely,
> Andrew Dell.

Luke crossed the street to the taxi rank, and attracted the attention of a driver.

"Allez au Hotel Tahiti, trouvez M. Andrew Dell; le portez au yacht Dorado, voilà! Comprenez-vous?"

"Oui, monsieur."

"Dépêchez-vous, s'il vous plaît."

"Oui, monsieur."

Luke summoned another driver. "Connaissez-vous Rolf Clute, qui demeure à Papeari?"

"Rolf Clute? Oui, monsieur. Tout le monde le connaît."

"Allez chez Rolf Clute; disez que c'est nécessaire qu'il vient avec vous au *yacht* Dorado *tout de suite. Comprenez-vous? Le* Dorado *c'est la grande goélette là.*"

"*Oui, monsieur.*"

Luke walked slowly back to the *Dorado*.

Something was wrong. He saw it in the faces of those aboard as he climbed the gangplank. All studied him with a curious detachment. To the rear stood Inspector Charles Duhamel, who once more bowed courteously. "A word with you, Mr. Royce, if you please."

McClure mumbled to Duhamel, "May we go now? There's no further point in our remaining."

"Another small moment or two, sir. Just possibly another item of information will be needed." He signaled Luke into the saloon. Luke entered, slowly took a seat. "What's going on?"

Duhamel stood with his knuckles pressed against the table-top. "Mr. Royce, I regret that I must bring a serious charge against you."

Luke leaned back in the chair, surveyed Duhamel with a grim smile. "On what basis?"

"On the day of Mr. Brady's death, your actions were observed by three independent witnesses. You came from the *Rahiria*, along the beach, to the outskirts of the *tamaraa*. There you quietly signaled Mr. Brady Royce, in a manner to suggest secrecy. You took him aside. Mr. Royce came back and said, 'I can't understand Luke. He is demented. He insists that I do not recognize him, that I do not tell anyone that he is here on the *Rahiria*, and then he makes me take a drink of wine. It is very strange.'

"Mr. Brady Royce repeated this statement to several persons. Immediately after, he became ill. The conclusions are unavoidable. What do you have to say to this, Mr. Royce?"

Luke laughed. "I'm delighted. You can't imagine how pleased I am."

Duhamel seemed hurt. "You are delighted? I fail to understand."

"You are convinced by the accusation?"

"It is verified by several persons."

"You have not yet heard what I have to tell you."

"No, of course not. You desired it so."

"Well then, bring everyone into the saloon. Everyone can listen."

"If you like." Duhamel went to the door. "Please, everyone into the saloon."

The passengers filed in from the afterdeck.

"I am sorry to inconvenience you," said Duhamel. "But Mr. Royce has a statement to make, which he feels will interest everyone."

McClure growled under his breath; Don Peppergold glared; Eiselhardt coolly lit a cigar.

"Proceed then, Mr. Royce."

"On Saturday, June 8 — this I believe was the date — I rode into Papeete on my motor-scooter. I went into the post office to get my mail. A man I then did not know but who I now know as Mr. Eiselhardt was waiting there, watching the post office boxes. The inference is that he knew my box number, but not where I lived. Later, when I had a chance to examine his passport I noticed that he had entered Papeete on June 5. I assume that he had been waiting in the post office every day. Inspector, this is a matter for you to verify. I am sure you'll be able to locate witnesses. Mr. Eiselhardt is a conspicuous man.

"He followed me from the post office…" Luke described the events of the day, his fall into the ocean, his bewilderment, his return to Papeete. "As I say, I was totally surprised. I could not understand why a stranger would want to kill me. This is why I did not report the affair to the police. The attempted murder would probably be dismissed as an accident; the murderer would be put on his guard. I shaved my beard, changed my clothes, and became James Harrison."

Luke started to describe his meeting with Carson, but was interrupted by the arrival aboard the *Dorado* of a tall lean man in a gray suit with a green turtle-neck shirt.

"Excuse me a moment," said Luke. He went out on deck, and the group inside the saloon saw him shake hands with the newcomer, exchange a few words, point up the waterfront. The man in the gray suit nodded, once more left the *Dorado*. Luke returned into the saloon. Charles Duhamel sat stiffly, his face frigid. The confrontation was proceeding along lines different from those he had envisioned. Eiselhardt sat relaxed, apparently indifferent, blowing small puffs of smoke into the air.

Luke watched Eiselhardt a moment, then continued. "There's not much I can tell you about Carson. He came aboard the *Rahiria* and Eiselhardt couldn't believe his good fortune — especially when Carson involved himself in a quarrel over a girl. Over the side went Carson.

No witnesses, no clues, no proof, nothing. Nothing, that is except a negative kind of proof. Eiselhardt and Carson shared a cabin. The ship was so crowded that any kind of a scuffle must have attracted attention. Only Eiselhardt had privacy enough to deal with Carson. I imagine he hit him over the head when Carson came into the cabin, waited until the coast was clear and slid him over the side. By morning, Carson was fifty miles astern.

"Now to Nuku Hiva. Eiselhardt leaves the *Rahiria*, goes to the post office. Someone has left a letter for him. Who? A mystery. Eiselhardt has an accomplice — someone who perhaps has planned the entire scheme.

"In fact, before we proceed any farther, perhaps we should consider the motivation behind these acts. Brady Royce was administrator of the Golconda Fund. Carson was next in line. Then me. If Carson and I were both dead, and lacking a male heir, Mrs. Lia Wintersea Royce would become administratrix.

"It would seem as if this were the plan: but perhaps I'm anticipating matters."

Luke looked out to the dock. "Well, look who's here. Some old friends, Mike Hannigan and Bob Higgins from the trimaran *Banshee*. Quite a gathering." Luke went to the door, called across to the dock. "Come on in, join the fun."

The Australians filed into the saloon, followed by the tall man in gray. Luke performed introductions. "Mike Hannigan, Bob Higgins, and this is my attorney Andrew Dell who has only just arrived from the United States. Gentlemen, we are discussing the murder of Brady Royce, and all of us are now pondering the identity of Ben Eiselhardt's accomplice. But again, perhaps I anticipate.

"At Hana Menu, the most beautiful bay of Hiva Oa, Brady commissioned a *tamaraa* for his guests. Everyone began eating. Ben Eiselhardt and two other witnesses state that I came over from the *Rahiria* and gave Brady a dose of poison."

"This is the case," said Eiselhardt in an even voice.

"In any event Brady was poisoned. He went aboard the *Dorado* and presently died. The doctor in attendance diagnosed fish poisoning, probably the toxic serum found in the *hue-hue*, or puffer fish."

Luke paused, rose to his feet, looked out along the waterfront. A taxi turned out of one of the side-streets, approached. Luke said, "I think that in a minute or so we'll have some expert testimony."

The taxi halted in front of the *Dorado*; Rolf Clute alighted. He saw Luke, gave a large wave of his hand. "Who's paying this taxi?"

"Tell him to wait. Come aboard. I need your help."

"Sure. What for?"

"A long story."

Rolf Clute came slowly up the gangplank, peered in surprise at the group in the saloon. "That's Duhamel in there. He's the gendarme!"

"Right. Some bad things have been happening." Luke led the way into the saloon. "This is Rolf Clute, who was aboard the *Rahiria* as far as Rangiroa. Rolf, you and Ben Eiselhardt went fishing in the Rangiroa lagoon, did you not?"

"Ben who? You mean Ben Easley? Him?" Rolf Clute pointed a long knobby finger.

"Yes. Did you go fishing with him?"

"Sure! Why not?"

"What did you catch?"

"Nothing much. Now that you mention it, he was interested in the *hue-hue*."

"Did you spear any?"

"Yeah, we got two."

"Then what?"

Rolf Clute licked his satyr's mouth, ran his hand through his shock of red hair. "Well, Ben asked me to show him the poison sac. I cut them up, pulled out the gland. Rest of the fish is good eating."

"Did Eiselhardt keep the sacs?"

"Eiselhardt — you mean Ben Easley again?"

"That's the name he was going by on the *Rahiria*."

"Well, Eiselhardt, Easley — whatever his name — I don't know what he did."

Luke addressed Duhamel. "For your information, Eiselhardt went spear-fishing by himself in the Tikehau lagoon. Perhaps he wanted to make sure that he had ample poison. Once at the *tamaraa* it was a simple matter to doctor Brady's plate, or perhaps pour a few drops of poison into a glass of toddy."

Eiselhardt spoke again, in the same even voice: "You lack all proof of this — just as you lack proof of your other accusations. Ask your lawyer, he'll tell you. So far it's guess-work."

"You and two others saw me come over from the *Rahiria* — that's better evidence?"

"Certainly."

"I see. Well, on Nuku Hiva I hired Mike and Bob to take me to Tai Oa Bay. The *Dorado* had departed; I was too late to save Brady's life. Along the way they told me that when they had ferried you to the *Dorado* that you had made a signal to one of the women aboard. They weren't sure which one; they saw nothing but her back. Right, Mike? Right, Bob?"

"Right." "Right."

"But she wore her hair in a tuft, eh?"

"Right again, all the way."

"Like one of the women in this room?"

"So right. Like her." Mike pointed.

"Yep. That's her," said Bob. "So far as I can prove from frontwards."

Luke turned to Charles Duhamel. "This is one of the witnesses who saw me approach Brady?"

"That is correct." Duhamel gnawed furiously at his mustache.

"I should mention," said Luke in an offhand voice, "that Mike and Bob took me to Hiva Oa aboard their trimaran. We arrived after the *tamaraa* was in progress, sometime after noon. Right, fellows?"

"Right." "Just so, matey."

"It becomes evident that Eiselhardt and his two witnesses gave the police false evidence. Mrs. Lia Royce of course was blackmailed; they had her totally in their power; they told her what to say. Is that correct, Lia?"

Lia, pale as milk, could only stare numbly. Her beauty was no longer real; it had vanished, giving way to a brittle white face.

"Just for the record: Mrs. McClure, do you ever wear your hair in a 'tuft' — a pony tail, that is?"

"Of course not," gasped Dorothy McClure.

"Kelsey — what about you?"

"Hah! With hair two inches long? No."

"Only Jean, then, wears her hair in a pony tail?"

"That's true," said Kelsey, examining Jean with sudden wonder.

Luke turned to Charles Duhamel. "There you have it: two murderers. They plotted to kill me. Eiselhardt drowned Carson, one or the other poisoned Brady. With Lia administrating the Golconda Fund, they were set for life." Luke paused to grin. "When I introduced myself as Luke Royce, this was the worst shock in their lives. Because they had failed. Never could they get the estate back to Lia. If I died, it would work its way through my branch of the family. They had lost — completely. All they could do was try to pin the killings on me and hope that a court would transfer the trusteeship back to Lia. Any questions, Inspector?"

"Yes, of course. Mrs. Royce, please tell me — is all this substantially true?"

"Yes," whispered Lia.

"Be quiet, you little fool!" shrieked Jean.

"What's the difference?" whispered Lia. "I've done nothing wrong — except lie for you to the police officer. You killed Brady — and poor Carson. I hope you hang."

"They had some kind of hold on you?" asked Duhamel.

"Yes. But nothing really disgraceful — just foolishness. In high school I became infatuated with Ben. He wanted me to live with him. I said no unless we were married. So he married me. It lasted two months. I wanted a divorce. He told me to forget it, that we never had been married to begin with, that he had been married to a girl named Inez Gallegos and had never got a divorce.

"A while later I became engaged to Brady. Inez was killed. I know what happened. Ben went to her for the marriage certificate. She wouldn't give it to him. He killed her and took the marriage certificate. Then I couldn't prove that we had not been married — that we were not still married. He began to humiliate me. He forced me to do things. Sleep with him. I even became pregnant. I didn't dare tell Brady, and I wanted to marry him. I know I should have been braver — but I'm not a brave woman."

Jean jumped to her feet, eyes staring, fingers clenched and bony. "Lia! Don't you dare say another word! Do you realize what you're doing?"

Lia nodded. "I'm just telling the truth."

Jean slowly sank back down in her chair.

"Lia was caught," said Luke. "Eiselhardt could demonstrate that he was married to her, that they had never been divorced. With Inez Gallegos dead and the marriage certificate in Eiselhardt's possession there was no way of proving otherwise — without going to an impossible amount of trouble. So anytime Eiselhardt wanted to do so he could invalidate Lia's marriage to Brady. Lia, I fear, lacked the fortitude to defy him, to tell Brady."

"I'm a coward," said Lia in a dreary voice. "I know it…There's nothing much more to tell," said Lia. "At Nuku Hiva, Jean told me that Ben was coming aboard, that I was to make it right with Brady. Which I did." She lowered her face into her hands. "I wish I had died along with him. I wish I were dead."

Luke spoke to Duhamel: "I asked Mr. Dell to get together what information he could and meet me here. I don't know what he has; I haven't had a chance to talk with him yet."

"In the main, corroboratory material," said Dell briskly. "It seems that Eiselhardt derived much of his income from pornographic movies. It's possible…" his eyes strayed toward Lia, then he looked away. "I suppose that aspect of the affair need not be pursued."

Duhamel rose to his feet. "Miss Wintersea, Mr. Eiselhardt: you have heard the accusation. What do you have to say?"

"Nothing, of course," said Ben Eiselhardt.

Luke said to Duhamel, "He waited for me in the post office three or four days. Find someone to identify him. He rented a Citroën; it must have been returned with a dent. Perhaps some of the natives at Tikehau saw him spearing *hue-hue*."

"Yes, yes," said Charles Duhamel in a haughty voice. "We are quite able to handle the details of our affairs. Miss Wintersea, Mr. Eiselhardt, you are under arrest."

Eiselhardt put a new cigar in his mouth, brought forth a large metal lighter.

"Look out," yelled McClure.

The lighter belched fire; a slug sang past Luke's ear.

Eiselhardt shook his head sadly. Don Peppergold sprang forward but Eiselhardt ignored him. He held the mechanism to his head. Once again there was an explosion and Ben Eiselhardt fell to the floor with a hole in his forehead.

CHAPTER XXI

THE *DORADO* WAS QUIET. The police had departed with Jean and the body of Ben Eiselhardt. Lia, the McClures and Don Peppergold had gone off to a hotel. Of the crew, only the stewards were aboard, packing Brady's personal effects for shipment to San Francisco.

Luke sat in the empty saloon watching twilight drift down upon the harbor. In spite of the events of the day, the saloon seemed peaceful and mellow. Luke felt at peace.

There was no immediate urgency for anything. Sooner or later he must return to San Francisco, but at the moment he felt disinclined to do anything but laze, to dawdle, to swim in cool blue lagoons, to explore remote white beaches.

No reason why he should not, of course. Here was the *Dorado*, ready to hand. Out across the Pacific were the Cook Islands, the seldom-visited Ellice group…

Steps sounded on the gangplank; female steps, brisk, light, yet somehow tentative.

Luke went to the door. It was Kelsey. "Oh, hello."

"Hello, Luke. I left my vanity case aboard."

"I suppose it's in your cabin."

"Yes. I suppose so…" She looked tentatively into the saloon. "You're sitting here all by yourself?"

"It's peaceful… Er, how about a glass of sherry?"

Kelsey gave a lame little laugh. "All right. In fact, that's why I came here."

"For sherry?"

"No. To talk a bit."

Luke poured sherry, handed a glass to Kelsey. "Sit down."

She sank upon one of the settees. "I want to apologize. Really I do. We were frightful to you—even when we knew you were guilty of nothing whatever."

"I understand. Say no more. Herd instinct: drive out the interloper."

"Partly that. And in my case, because I'm perverse and malicious. I know it. I deceive other people, like my mother and father and Don, but I don't deceive myself."

"All right. You're no good. I believe you."

"I came here to beguile you. I know I can do that too."

"All right. I'm beguiled. It's pleasant for a change. I like it. But why?"

"Shall I be utterly candid?"

"You won't offend me."

Kelsey slid a foot closer along the settee. "I don't want to go home. I don't intend to go. Mother and Father are flying out as soon as the police take their depositions. Don—I don't know. There may be a scene. Still, if he can't find me he can't argue or bluster…What will you do?"

Luke gave a small dry chuckle. "I'm taking a vacation—aboard the *Dorado*. I'm sailing out into the middle of the Pacific."

Kelsey sipped her sherry, cocked her head sidewise. "I rather thought you might…Can I come along?"

Luke looked up at the ceiling. "I don't know whether I want company or not. Or what kind of company."

Kelsey moved several inches closer.

"I wouldn't be in the way," she said earnestly. "And think: shuffleboard. Wouldn't you rather play shuffleboard with me than old Sarvis?"

"Sarvis comes in a poor second. No question about it."

"Luke—do you consider me extremely forward?"

"Well, yes. I do."

"For a very good reason. I am that. May I have more sherry?"

"Of course. Pour for me too, if you will."

"With pleasure. You see, I can do things, like pouring sherry."

Luke watched her. Fetching, beyond doubt: charming, provocative. Perhaps too much so. Luke again considered the ceiling.

Kelsey clinked glasses. "To set matters perfectly straight," she said softly, "I am not a cold-blooded opportunist. Certainly not cold-blooded, at any rate."

They sat in silence for a moment or two, watching the lights twinkle into existence across old Papeete.

"It's been dreadful," whispered Kelsey. "But I wouldn't have missed it for the world."

"You knew Eiselhardt in high school?"

"I never could tolerate him. Only weak-minded girls like Lia and Inez liked Ben. He was so obviously twisted and cruel...But let's not talk about the past. Can I come with you?"

Luke drew a deep sigh. "You catch me at a weak moment. I want someone to soothe me, to stroke my head, to pour me sherry from time to time."

"And Sarvis doesn't do it the right way?"

"He doesn't know the first thing about it."

Kelsey touched a finger to his forehead. "It feels like it might be nice to stroke. I'll be ever so careful."

"I don't want any scenes with your family. I don't want to fight Don Peppergold."

"I'll handle everything. That's included in the soothing part. All you have to do is play the ukulele and pay for running the boat."

"Oddly enough," said Luke, "I can do both. Well, then, another glass of sherry and after that —"

"After that," said Kelsey, "I will be going ashore. Otherwise you'd think I was worse than I really am. And I'm really not bad at all. Not too bad. I just want to visit those far-away islands."

"I hope I'm not called to San Francisco on an important matter," said Luke. "Then you'd have to start all over again, beguiling Sarvis."

"Sarvis is really an old dear," said Kelsey. "Perhaps he might like to be petted and soothed too."

"Please, not on the same ship." Luke rose to his feet. "Are you hungry?"

"Starving."

"Way out around the island, at Taravao, there's a restaurant. It's called the Atchoun. Shall we go there for dinner?"

"I'd love to."

✳

Candles flickered to the airs drifting in from hibiscus bushes. Looking across the table, Luke thought, I wonder what I'm getting into? Whatever it is, it can't be all bad.

Kelsey spoke. "Luke."

"Yes."

"You're thinking of something."

"I realize that."

"And I know what it is. Never, never, never, would I marry you."

" 'Never' is a long time," said Luke.

"Never, never, never is even longer. Do you know why I wouldn't?"

"First of all, I haven't asked you."

"No. It's nothing like that. It's because of this. Right now you're in a stage of nervous reaction. After a while, you'd start thinking. You never could trust me. Not really. You'd never forget how I acted when you were all alone and everyone was against you. Would you?" She searched his face.

Luke reviewed a dozen answers, found pitfalls everywhere. He said at last, "People are dead. Others are miserable. Don Peppergold is angry. But for me, and perhaps for you — everything is pleasant. So why should I complain?"

Kelsey smiled and looked into the candles. "You didn't answer my question."

"No."

"Perhaps it's just as well."

About the Author

Jack Vance was born in 1916 to a well-off California family that, as his childhood ended, fell upon hard times. As a young man he worked at a series of unsatisfying jobs before studying mining engineering, physics, journalism and English at the University of California Berkeley. Leaving school as America was going to war, he found a place as an ordinary seaman in the merchant marine. Later he worked as a rigger, surveyor, ceramicist, and carpenter before his steady production of sf, mystery novels, and short stories established him as a full-time writer.

His output over more than sixty years was prodigious and won him three Hugo Awards, a Nebula Award, a World Fantasy Award for lifetime achievement, as well as an Edgar from the Mystery Writers of America. The Science Fiction and Fantasy Writers of America named him a grandmaster and he was inducted into the Science Fiction Hall of Fame.

His works crossed genre boundaries, from dark fantasies (including the highly influential *Dying Earth* cycle of novels) to interstellar space operas, from heroic fantasy (the *Lyonesse* trilogy) to murder mysteries featuring a sheriff (the Joe Bain novels) in a rural California county. A Vance story often centered on a competent male protagonist thrust into a dangerous, evolving situation on a planet where adventure was his daily fare, or featured a young person setting out on a perilous odyssey over difficult terrain populated by entrenched, scheming enemies.

Late in his life, a world-spanning assemblage of Vance aficionados came together to return his works to their original form, restoring material cut by editors whose chief preoccupation was the page count of a pulp magazine. The result was the complete and authoritative *Vance Integral Edition* in 44 hardcover volumes. Spatterlight Press is now publishing the VIE texts as ebooks, and as print-on-demand paperbacks.

Colophon

This book was printed using Adobe Arno Pro as the primary text font, with NeutraFace used on the cover.

This title was created from the digital archive of the Vance Integral Edition, a series of 44 books produced under the aegis of the author by a worldwide group of his readers. The VIE project gratefully acknowledges the editorial guidance of Norma Vance, as well as the cooperation of the Department of Special Collections at Boston University, whose John Holbrook Vance collection has been an important source of textual evidence.

Special thanks to R.C. Lacovara, Patrick Dusoulier, Koen Vyverman, Paul Rhoads, Chuck King, Gregory Hansen, Suan Yong, and Josh Geller for their invaluable assistance preparing final versions of the source files.

Source: Paul Rhoads; Digitize: Richard Chandler, Jurriaan Kalkman, Gan Uesli Starling, Billy Webb; Format: Lori Hanley; Diff: David A. Kennedy, David Reitsema; Tech Proof: Bob Moody; Text Integrity: Patrick Dusoulier, Tim Stretton, Suan Hsi Yong; Implement: Derek W. Benson, Hans van der Veeke; Security: Tim Stretton; Compose: John A. Schwab; Comp Review: Christian J. Corley, Charles King, Bob Luckin, Robin L. Rouch; Update Verify: Robert Melson, Paul Rhoads, Robin L. Rouch; RTF-Diff: Charles King; Textport: Patrick Dusoulier; Proofread: Michel Bazin, Malcolm Bowers, Patrick Dusoulier, Harry Erwin, Ed Gooding, Peter Ikin, Jody Kelly, David A. Kennedy, Chris McCormick, Bob Moody, Till Noever, Axel Roschinski, Bill Sherman, Mark Shoulder

Artwork (maps based on original drawings by Jack and Norma Vance):

Paul Rhoads, Christopher Wood

Book Composition and Typesetting: Joel Anderson

Art Direction and Cover Design: Howard Kistler

Proofing: Christian J. Corley, Steve Sherman

Jacket Blurb: John Vance

Management: John Vance, Koen Vyverman

www.ingramcontent.com/pod-product-compliance
Lightning Source LLC
Chambersburg PA
CBHW031128210626
46816CB00015B/1207